THE STONES
and the Shaman

Claire Whatley

Published in 2008 by YouWriteOn.com

First Edition

Published by YouWriteOn.com

CHAPTER ONE
The Speaking Stone

May 1955

Ingrid's legs ached, her chest ached and she was disgustingly sweaty. Her fine, straight, brown hair stuck to the back of her neck. She had thought this would be easy. Anyway, at least the effort of the climb might help her work off her anger. Parents! They drove her mad! If Dad and Mother were determined to ignore her, then they would not notice her going off, would they?

She had wanted to reach the strange statue at the top of the hill - this was where she would capture the best view – but the rocks kept sliding away from under her. She was making no progress at all. She sat down on a rock, gingerly, making sure it was stable, then stretched out her legs. It was good to feel alone and free after all the travelling. The jagged mass of the snow-capped Himalayan range stretched across the horizon before her. Behind her, she could see the campsite way below, and her parents like little mechanical toys, popping in and out of their tent while the Sherpas tended the yaks. They all looked so busy. She took off her rucksack and reached in for her sketchbook and pencils.

From somewhere above her, a small rock fell, landing by her feet. Probably knocked by a mountain goat. She could not be bothered to turn round to look. She pushed her hair off her face and concentrated on the view before her, sketchbook on lap, pencil poised.

The complicated pattern of barbs, spikes and strange angles that made up the Himalaya needed to be stared at long and hard before pencil could touch paper. As she stared, she forgot her resentment.

Suddenly, another stone of the same size landed near her, to her left. This was no accident. The stone had been thrown. Ingrid felt her heart beating, loud and fast. She rose quickly from the rock, dropping her sketchbook and pencil, and spinning round on her heels, nearly falling as she did so. As she turned, she faced into the dazzling mid-afternoon sun, and for a moment it was hard to see anything at all. Apart from circling vultures high above, all was still. Was one of the younger Sherpas playing a trick on her? It seemed unlikely – they both seemed painfully shy.

How dare anyone throw stones at her? Perhaps it was just local kids teasing a foreigner. Also unlikely – the nearest village must be at least four miles away. She began to walk up and across to the left, picking her way over the loose stones. She was aware that she was moving right out of sight of the camp. She could hear someone call quietly in a sing-song, nasal, feminine voice in some language that wasn't Nepali. She stopped to listen, her ears straining to hear above the sound of her thumping heart.

There it was again, from behind a dense patch of scrub. Definitely a female voice, but a language unlike anything Ingrid had ever heard, quietly ranging through the octaves, but mostly comprising high squeaks and "ooo" sounds. Her heart felt as though it was swelling with every thudding beat, taking up her entire chest cavity. With a mad, brave impulse, she spoke,

"Hello? Who is it?"

"Hellooo," replied the singsong voice.

It sounded friendly, but why was this person hiding and trying to lead her away from the camp? There was a terrified part of Ingrid screaming within her, telling her to head back down to the camp as fast as she could, even if it meant sliding down the scree most of the way and probably injuring herself. Somehow she ignored the impulse, and instead crept round the scrub and forced herself speak in a calm voice,

"Hello? Who's there?"

The Speaking Stone

As she came round the dense, thorny bushes, the sight which met her eyes made her dizzy with shock, fear and curiosity. A creature stood before her, at least a foot taller than her own height, almost covered in pale blond hair. Its mainly hairless face had a long chin and prominent cheeks: something like an orang-utan; but its skin looked very soft: something like a human. Its arms were long, but it stood erect. Its large blue eyes were staring into Ingrid's green ones. The stare was so intense it made Ingrid blink. It was motionless for a moment, then it opened its mouth to reveal its enormous yellow teeth, held a hand to its chest and said, "Kol-pa."

Ingrid knew exactly what she was looking at. Only last year, 1954, one of the national newspapers had sent out an expedition to the Himalaya, attempting to find these very creatures. Gigantopithecus. The yeti.

Ingrid's legs were wobbling crazily from sheer terror, and she felt faint. She also felt so sick she truly feared she might vomit. It was as though the muscles in her legs had melted. She *could not* run. She half sat, half fell onto a nearby rock, never taking her eyes from the creature.

The yeti calmly imitated her by sitting on a nearby rock. They sat facing each other, about two feet apart; Ingrid trembling uncontrollably. The yeti held something in one hand. It reached across towards Ingrid and slowly opened up its hand to reveal a breathtakingly beautiful gemstone, the size of a quail's egg, gleaming blue and purple with the intensity and lustre of a thousand dragonflies. The stone itself seemed to be compelling Ingrid to take it. With a massive surge of will, battling her faintness and terror, she took the stone. As she took it, she felt the smooth warm hairless palm of the yeti's hand. She stopped shaking almost as soon as the stone was in her grasp. Her faintness and nausea began to ease. Reassurance seemed to be flowing into her from the stone itself. The yeti began to speak. Ingrid found she could understand every word.

The Stones and the Shaman

"My name is Kol-pa. I am six years old, which is nearly grown-up. I am a girl, and I think you are a girl, too, even though your clothes seem like those of a human male. You understand me because you hold a Speaking Stone. If you give it back to me, you can tell me about yourself and where you come from and I will understand you."

Ingrid passed back the stone, once more touching the steady warmth of Kol-pa's hand as she did so. As the stone left her, adrenalin pumped once more through Ingrid's body, urging her to run. She resisted and said,

"I'm Ingrid. I'm eleven and, yes, of course I'm a girl. I'm camping down there with my parents. They're on an expedition to find new plants. We only arrived here today. We come from England – that's a country a very long way away. We've travelled by train and boat and...," it occurred to her that this creature might well have no knowledge of trains and boats, and that she was saying anything that came into her head in a sort of panic, so she tried to deflect the conversation back to the yeti-girl, "Are you..." Ingrid's speech trailed off. She wanted to say "real", "friendly", "alone" and "a yeti" all at once, but she realised any of those things would have sounded rude and might antagonise the creature - and without that incredible stone, she was feeling alarmingly weak and vulnerable.

Kol-pa returned the stone, laughing a strange nasal laugh,

"Yes, I am a yeti – as you would say – and of course I am friendly. The humans who live here call us meh-teh," Kol-pa paused thoughtfully, once again staring disconcertingly into Ingrid's eyes, "Is England in the West?"

Ingrid nodded, rendered speechless for a moment by the realisation that this creature appeared to have read her mind. There was another pause, then,

"I live with all my family a little way from here. Would you like to meet some of them?" and then, as an afterthought she added, "They are friendly, like me."

The Speaking Stone

Clutching the stone, Ingrid thought of all the excellent reasons for returning at once to the camp, but found herself saying,

"Yes!"

CHAPTER TWO
The Yeti Cave

As they walked along, Ingrid' worries seemed to drift away. She smiled up at Kol-pa, feeling wonderfully protected. She didn't care in the least whether she was experiencing fantasy or reality. It was like the best of dreams. She felt completely safe.

However, she *was* tired and the difficult terrain was beginning to feel painfully real. Ingrid struggled to clamber over bigger and increasingly unstable rocks. After half an hour of walking and scrambling, Ingrid's wool trousers, thick socks and heavy boots were making her so hot she felt on the verge of combustion. Her cotton shirt stuck to her underneath her wool sweater. She felt sweaty and itchy. Meanwhile, Kol-pa bounded across the rocks easily on all fours, using her knuckles in a gorilla-like way. Ingrid gasped in the thin air. Suddenly, Kol-pa stopped.

"Hop onto my back!"

Ingrid hesitated. Two bleating goats, a mother and kid, watched them from above, on a narrow ledge of rock. Kol-pa crouched down,

"Go on!"

The mother goat bleated again, watching them. Ingrid climbed on to Kol-pa's warm, soft back. Kol-pa hoisted her up higher so that Ingrid could put her arms around the thick fur of her neck. Ingrid still held the purple stone in her left hand. Kol-pa held on to Ingrid's legs, bounded off almost as fast as before, now on two legs, and began to speak,

"While we are going along like this we can speak to each other easily without exchanging the Speaking Stone. The stone's energy flowing into you can reach me as long as we touch, you see? I will tell you about the meh-teh."

“We have lived on the planet you call Earth for much longer than humans, but my family and our relatives in the Himalaya are now the only meh-teh left in the world. Long ago, our kind lived in other high places of this planet. We all knew each other regardless of the distances that separated us because we could talk to each other with our minds."

"Can you read my mind?" interrupted Ingrid.

Kol-pa laughed, "A little, but it is not easy as human minds are so muddled. It's one of the things the Speaking Stone seems to help with, though."

"Could I read your mind, then?"

"As far as I know, this is not something ordinary humans can do - but who knows? Perhaps the Stone will help you with this. But for now, I must speak to you with the voice you can hear. There is so much you need to know. I must tell you the story of the meh-teh.”

“Since the time human beings began to multiply fast, there have been fewer and fewer safe places for the meh-teh, so that these mountains are now our last home in the world.”

“But why is it not safe for you?” asked Ingrid in an indignant tone, “Human beings don’t even realise you exist!”

“The mountain people here know of us, but out of fear or respect, they leave us alone. Most of your species is not like this. They are insatiably curious and greedy. Many Western humans suspect that we exist, and will not rest until they find us. Once we are found, there will be no peace for us. You would eventually destroy us, whether by intention or accident. We must not allow this to happen. We must never be found…”

“But you let me find you!”

"You are going to help us. *I* had to find *you*. You are the one who has come here to save us from the rest of your kind and from one man in particular. This is your quest. This is why you are coming with me now."

"What man? What quest? I don't know what you are talking about - I just came here because my parents are plant-hunters. How could I have come here for you? I didn't know you existed either!"

Feeling nervous and defensive, Ingrid began to wonder whether her parents would actually have missed her yet. She doubted that her father would, but her mother might, and that gave her a momentary pang of anxiety. Despite the benign effect of the stone and Kol-pa's apparent friendliness, Ingrid felt threatened, and very alone. She must have been utterly *mad* to come all this way on the back of some kind of talking gorilla. She needed to climb down off this weird beast's back and run for her life to the safety of the camp. However, there was no time for Ingrid to plan an escape because at that moment, Kol-pa, who was holding onto Ingrid with an iron grip, came to an abrupt stop.

"You are about to find out, Ingrid. We are here!"

The yeti cave would have been completely invisible to any human eye. As they approached it, it seemed to Ingrid that they were walking straight into a thicket of scrub in between a maze of rocks. Ingrid had to close her eyes as Kol-pa carried her through, and she ducked her head down to avoid being scratched. The cave smelled of clean straw, earthy vegetables and wood fires. As Kol-pa contorted her body to enter the cave, Ingrid slipped slightly down her back. Kol-pa heaved her up again in a sharp, sudden unexpected move, and Ingrid dropped the stone.

As it hit the dusty dry cave floor with a thud, all Ingrid's exhaustion and fear, her aching limbs, the hurt in her chest, flooded through her in an overwhelming sensation of homesickness and desolation. She lost consciousness.

* * *

The Yeti Cave

The first sensation to reach Ingrid's awareness as she woke was a mouth-watering smell, like pancakes. She could visualise their creamy-brown speckled surfaces, the sprinkling of caster sugar, the squeeze of lemon.

In a dream-like state from the warm comfort of her resting place, she thought at that moment she was in her bed at home. There was her blue willow patterned wallpaper; her framed painting of Henry, her fox terrier; her candlewick bedspread in blue, yellow and white – home at last! It was morning and there were pancakes for breakfast. Wonderful!

She opened her eyes to the unwelcome realisation that this was not her home, not her bed, not even the camp. In her wildest dreams or nightmares nothing could have been less like her own home. On the walls surrounding her were row upon row of gemstones, in every shade of purple, blue and green, on rock-cut shelves, sparkling in the light of a fire blazing in the centre of a vast cavern. She turned her head to the left and gasped in shock as her eyes suddenly met two pale blue eyes, without any visible white, in a massive, impassive, wrinkled brown face. The face, surrounded by blond hair, streaked white, was smiling. There was no hint of malice in the face: it looked kind and caring.

Ingrid was lying on a squishy mattress, covered by some sort of divinely soft blanket, and on the blanket, resting on the region of her solar plexus were three stones: the purple Speaking Stone she had dropped earlier, another one, deep yew-tree green, and one palest shimmering violet. Her chest felt fine and her legs had lost their ache.

"Have something to eat, my dear," said a voice from below the pale blue eyes. Another pair of eyes came into focus, much brighter blue: Kol-pa. Ingrid noticed that both yeti had a small Speaking Stone worn as a pendant on a piece of twine around their necks.

"Yes, eat it up," said Kol-pa, encouragingly, "You will really like it!"

Ingrid was being offered a plate made of some sort of tree bark, on which lay strips of root vegetable, which had the look of having been cooked over an open fire, a little charred, with a shiny glaze on them. Slowly, she sat up. The stones rolled off her chest, but remained on the blanket, resting on her legs. Her head throbbed as she moved. As she reached for the plate, she saw that her fingers were swollen.

"You have a little mountain sickness, my dear. You humans from the lowlands should be careful when you come to our mountains. You will be fine. The green stone is helping the mountain sickness to go away, and the violet stone is relieving your tiredness. You must eat, drink and rest," said the older yeti.

Ingrid ate. Kol-pa was right. She really liked it. It was sweet-sour and blissfully filling. She devoured the food greedily, picking it up with her slightly numb fingers. Although she had drunk plenty of Nepali tea since their arrival at camp, she had eaten very little and was now ravenous. She had a wonderfully happy, protected feeling like the moment you wake up after a long illness, surrounded by your family. Kol-pa and the other yeti laughed, gratified to see Ingrid's enjoyment of their food. When she had finished eating, Kol-pa gave her cool water to drink from a large hollowed-out seed-pod.

As she was drinking, a figure suddenly leapt up in front of her, making hideous, deafening roaring and shrieking sounds. Ingrid screamed in panic, dropping the seed-pod, spilling water all over the blanket and herself, instinctively grabbing Kol-pa for protection. Kol-pa began to speak at once in angry tones, and the roaring creature dissolved into chimpanzee-like shrieks of laughter, rolling around on the floor.

"Forgive him, Ingrid. It is only my baby brother, Ketu. He is just two years old, and still very childish. I am very sorry he alarmed you," said Kol-pa, sympathetically.

"Ketu, come here and say hello to the human girl, Ingrid," said the other yeti and she continued, "Forgive me also. I have not told you who I am. My name is Mamo. I am the grandmother of Kol-pa and Ketu. You will see the rest of our family at another time, because soon we must return you to your camp. There is much I have to tell you and much you have to learn, but you needed to rest for so long that now your mother is beginning to worry. Your porters will soon be searching for you."

Ingrid mumbled embarrassed thanks to Mamo as Ketu shambled across to her with a sheepish look.

"Hello," he said, gently stroking her arm, and nuzzling his soft cheek against her shoulder. His eyes were dark blue and gleamed with mischief. He had long dark eyelashes which contrasted strikingly with his pale, platinum blond coat. His expression, both angelic and devilish, seemed to be appealing to Ingrid for forgiveness, but whether he was genuine or mocking, she could not tell. She did not much like or understand small children, human or otherwise. She had no experience of them. She only had two older brothers: James, who was twenty, and Richard, aged eighteen, who was just about to start his National Service (whenever she thought of National Service it made her so glad to be a girl). She gave Ketu a brief, grudging half-smile - not yet forgiving him for terrifying her, soaking her and making her look stupid - and turned away.

Mamo took the gemstones from Ingrid's lap, putting the purple one in her hand, then eased her up from the bed to a standing position.

"You are well enough to return now, and Kol-pa can carry ... on part of the descent so that you will quickly be with your ... r and father again. Your bag and drawing materials are where you left them. Kol-pa will take you that far. Do not speak of what you have seen. There is still much you need to know. I will come to you tonight."

"Oh, well, thank you, but I don't know if my parents will..."

"Don't worry. Your parents will not know. I will come."

"No, you don't understand. You can't..."

"I will come."

Ingrid imagined the scene if this enormous aged yeti were to turn up in the middle of the night in the tent she shared with her parents, but it was clear she could not argue with Mamo.

Kol-pa hoisted Ingrid onto her back, saying,

"It's fun carrying you - you are so light – I don't know you're there!"

"Well, I know I'm a bit thin, but I am tall for my age," replied Ingrid, defensively. She had always been sensitive about her skinny build, and the extraordinary bulk and strength of these hominids emphasised her own fragility.

As they moved swiftly through numerous cavern rooms, Ingrid was spell-bound by the endless shelves of precious looking gems shimmering around the walls. Most of the rooms had no other light source than that which came from the stones themselves.

"What do you do with all these stones, Kol-pa?"

"Just about everything. They are our medicine, our science, our history, our future. I suppose you could say they are our books and these rooms are our libraries."

"I don't understand what you mean."

"You will," laughed Kol-pa.

The cave walls without shelves were covered in swirling, dream-like murals. Ketu accompanied them to the exit of the cave, making ape-like sounds interspersed with chimp-like hoots and the occasional intelligible word. As Ingrid and Kol-pa left, Ketu stood at the door, smiling, fidgeting and waving good-bye, just like any other little child.

* * *

As they approached the place where Ingrid had left her art materials, Kol-pa made a sound something like, "Uh-oh." The rhythmic rocking on Kol-pa's back had lulled Ingrid into a half-sleep, but she awoke with a jolt at the yeti's exclamation, saying,

"What? What's wrong?"

Ingrid hauled herself higher up Kol-pa's back to see ahead, as they came to a stop. A mountain goat was standing before them, Ingrid's rucksack dangling by a strap from its mouth as it chewed peacefully, its eyes glazed. Ingrid slid off Kol-pa's back and raced to the goat, arms flailing,

"Hey, get off! Get off, you dim-witted animal! Off! Off!"

The goat had clearly never been addressed in this way before and as a precautionary measure, took a few paces back, still chewing the rucksack strap. Ingrid made a grab for re-possession and after a brief tug-of-war, which the goat clearly enjoyed, he let go and trotted off. Kol-pa was applauding and laughing behind her, saying something unintelligible. Ingrid realised she had dropped the Speaking Stone. Kol-pa spoke again and reached down to retrieve it. She handed it back to Ingrid.

"Just keep it in your pocket. It will still have the same effect. You will need it when Mamo comes. You know your way now from here, don't you?"

"Yes, of course I do," said Ingrid, in a sharper voice than she had intended, slipping the stone into her trouser pocket and then collecting up her pencils from the ground, "but when will I see you again?"

"You'll come back tomorrow. As early as you can – we don't have much time."

"Well, I don't know if I can – it depends what my parents are doing, and what mood they're in. If they're furious with me when I get back now, there's not much chance of their allowing me out on my own tomorrow," replied Ingrid, hoisting her mangled pack on to her back. The chewed strap was still just about whole, but coated disgustingly with white trails of goat saliva. She wiped her hands on her trousers.

"Ingrid, just don't worry. Mamo will tell you everything tonight. And you *will* come tomorrow – it's your destiny. I must go now."

Without another word, Kol-pa bounded off and was quickly out of sight.

"I don't want a destiny," said Ingrid, quietly, as she slowly turned round and began her descent back to the camp.

CHAPTER THREE
A Tooth

As Ingrid approached the large, green army tent she shared with her parents, she heard their voices: her father's loud and exasperated; her mother's, soft and concerned. She paused to listen.

"Look, we made the decision to bring her with us. Now she is here, we either allow her to be a free spirit and explore on her own, or we keep her by our side at all times. You know that would bore her to death as well as being hugely detrimental to our work."

"David, she has been gone for more than three hours…"

"I'm sure it's nearer two."

"I'm telling you it's over *three*. Anyway, it's *too long*. We must go out now to look for her. She could have fallen and broken a bone. She could be hopelessly lost…attacked by a leopard…anything. We cannot just sit here and wait. Imagine if she is lost or injured."

"Alright, it's against my better judgment, but I'll send one of the Sherpas. There is absolutely no point in either of us wasting our brief time here on a wild goose chase. When she is back, we must speak to her and establish a few rules for the duration of this camp. Listen, Celia, we both know this is a prime location for entirely new species, and we cannot waste our sponsorship running around after Ingrid. The sooner she goes to boarding school the better."

Ingrid's mother's eyes were slowly welling with tears as Ingrid lifted the tent flap. She entered and two voices, one furious, one frantic said,

"Ingrid!"

All three began speaking at once.

"Hello, Mother. Hello, Dad. I've been for a long walk and…"

"Ingrid – it's been three hours – we've been so…"

"Now listen to me, Ingrid, we need to establish a few…"

"LISTEN!" cried out Ingrid's mother. She so rarely raised her voice, that Ingrid and her father listened.

"We are all tired, hungry and thirsty. It's been an exhausting journey from Kathmandu, and I for one am developing a raging headache. Ingrid, the fact of the matter is, you are back, apparently safe and well. There will be time tomorrow to discuss your comings and goings during our stay here. I can smell that Tshering is preparing supper, so let's just drink some tea, eat supper and retire to our sleeping bags early. You can tell us about your adventures over supper."

Ingrid's stomach gave a momentary lurch of panic at the thought of supper following all the food she had stuffed down in the yeti cave. She would have to make an effort.

"Mother, you mustn't worry about me. I am nearly twelve, you know! I'm used to exploring by myself. You and Dad wouldn't want me following you around, getting in the way."

"Ingrid is right – she must be allowed a degree of independence. You're right, too, Celia – we need supper. Let's see how Tshering is getting on."

It was unusual for her father to be so conciliatory, so Ingrid wisely said no more. Besides, she needed thinking time to invent a story of her activities over the last three hours. They emerged from the tent to find Tshering approaching to tell them in his quiet, heavily accented voice, that supper was indeed ready.

A Tooth

The Wildsmiths had five Sherpas with them on this stage of the expedition. Tshering, who was about forty, was the cook; quiet and dependable.

Pasang was the most senior, both in years and experience. He was extraordinarily wrinkled and Ingrid found it hard to tell his age. He could have been anything between fifty and seventy. He had been their guide to this camp, in the heart of a botanically rich area of the Himalayan foothills. He spoke English well, and rarely stopped talking, but his accent was so strong that Ingrid often had difficulty understanding him. If she politely pretended to understand him, he could always tell she had not understood a word. It made him laugh in a way that embarrassed her horribly.

And then, there was Pemba. He also appeared to be respected as a senior. He was a kindly-faced man in his mid-forties. He was quiet, but very knowledgeable about the local flora. He and Pasang would be guiding Ingrid's parents on their daily research expeditions. According to Pasang, his own name meant Friday, and Pemba's name meant Saturday. Ingrid had been intrigued by this idea, but disappointed to find that the other Sherpas did not have names relating to days of the week.

The boys, Ketsun and Sonam, looked after the yaks, and generally did as they were told by the others. It was hard to tell their age because they were both fairly small, especially Ketsun. Ingrid guessed they were both about fourteen or fifteen. They did not appear to speak much English, but chatted away quietly to each other in the Sherpa language.

The eight of them sat around the fire companionably, all eating rice and dhal with their fingers in the traditional manner. Pasang usually had a great deal to say at meal-times. On this occasion, Ingrid went hot with the consciousness of her secret as he began to tell a tale of the meh-teh, who, he assured them, were occasionally seen in this area.

"So have you ever seen one of these creatures yourself, Pasang?" asked Ingrid's father in a sardonic tone.

"Oh yes, Mr. Wildsmith, oh yes. But only from a distance, usually at dusk. They are big, big creatures, much taller even than you. They have light-coloured hair, a little like this," he gestured to the sleeve of Ingrid's Aran sweater, "Also, I have seen their footprints. They are huge, Mr. Wildsmith, huge," he gestured the size of the footprint with his hands. "They are shy animals, so they usually search for food at dusk, or in the early part of the night. They are mainly vegetarian, but if they are really hungry they will eat meat. Oh yes! So beware, Miss Ingrid, they would gobble you up in two bites!" he laughed.

Ingrid managed to laugh, but her laughter sounded hollow. She noticed Sonam staring at her, but he quickly looked away as her eyes met his.

"Oh really, Pasang, you are just trying to frighten us," said Ingrid's mother, "I think that's quite enough!"

"No, Mrs. Wildsmith, it is true – the meh-teh are real," he leaned forward confidentially and lowered his voice, "I have a tooth."

He drew from his pocket something which did look exactly like an enormous molar, and held it in his open palm for the edification of his audience. It was over an inch long, creamy-white and in good condition. No-one could be in any doubt that it was a real tooth.

Pemba seemed to disapprove of this and said something quietly to Pasang in rapid Sherpa. Pasang answered him in a soothing tone. Ingrid's heart lurched and she let out a gasp as she found she understood what they were saying. It was something like,

"You have too much to say to the Westerners, Pasang - just leave it, and put that thing away."

"Calm down, calm down - they're too dim to believe it, anyway, aren't they?"

Tshering added something, obviously siding with Pemba, but he was too quiet for Ingrid to hear. She was frozen with shock at the power of the small stone in her pocket. Sonam had seen her reaction. He had a strange look, almost as though he was suppressing a smile.

"Where did you find this, Pasang?" interrupted Mr. Wildsmith, clearly intrigued despite his scepticism.

"If you spend much time in the mountains, these are not hard to find. I keep it for luck and while I have it, the meh-teh will never harm me."

"Well, Pasang, whatever that object may be, mountaineers and explorers have been coming here from our country for years, and I have never heard of any ending up as a yeti supper," said Mrs. Wildsmith.

"Exactly, Mrs. Wildsmith," he replied, putting the tooth away, "The meh-teh feel frightened by so many people invading their homeland now, you see. It makes creatures more dangerous when they are frightened. Oh yes, I am serious. They are at peace with the Sherpas and the Nepali and Tibetan people, but they are frightened of all you Western invaders! You must be careful!"

"Well," said Mr.Wildsmith, "I accept that the Himalayas are all the rage since Hillary and Norgay, but they are hardly overcrowded. It's all good for your business, of course, even if the yeti do not approve. However, they have little to fear from us. We are simply here on a peaceable plant-finding mission. We will leave yeti-hunting to the sensationalising British press and gullible Hollywood film-stars. Anyway, I think you are frightening my daughter. Ingrid, are you alright? You're very quiet. You've hardly eaten."

"I'm fine, Dad, I'm just tired."

"Actually, I think we're all pretty tired," said Mrs. Wildsmith, "but why don't you tell us about what *you* got up to this afternoon? We were terribly worried about you, you know."

"Er, well," said Ingrid, panicking, "it was nothing very exciting – I was sketching and I lost all track of the time. I really am so tired – shall I tell you about it tomorrow?"

"Yes, of course, dear, and show us your sketches, too," replied her mother, "You look quite pale. I think we should all go to bed early – it's getting so cold now, anyway. Come on, up you get. Thank you for a wonderful meal, Tshering," she said, turning to the cook, who responded by placing his palms together in front of his forehead in the traditional way.

"Yes, thank you, Tshering, that was excellent," added Ingrid's father as they all began to get up to make ready for bed. The Sherpas began to busy themselves, putting out the camp fire and taking away the metal plates to be washed. As the Wildsmiths went to clean their teeth, wash and to relieve themselves at the makeshift latrines, Ingrid tried to order her racing thoughts. Pasang's words conflicted with the reality she had seen, but on the other hand, didn't peaceful creatures have a right to defend themselves against invaders? And Mamo was coming to her tonight...

CHAPTER FOUR
Demons

"I hadn't realised it would be like this! Why was I so worried! Why am I *always* so worried?!" thought Ingrid, smiling happily to herself, "Here I am sitting – who knows where - with a giant yeti granny in the middle of the night, and Mother and Dad know nothing about it. Incredible!"

"My dear Ingrid," began Mamo softly in a tone that immediately erased Ingrid's smile, making her feel sad, and very young, "there is great danger here. That is why I am speaking to you now in this way, in your dream. Do not forget what I am saying to you. There is danger for the meh-teh, but there is also danger for you and your family. I am sorry to give you the burden of this secret, but the meh-teh's time here is drawing to an end, and the Prophecy tells us that a girl of your species – that *you* - will one day tell our story to the world."

Mamo's wrinkled brown face was filled with sadness and kindness. Her enormous hand reached across to hold Ingrid's right hand.

"There is a human – a shaman – who wishes to destroy us in order to steal the secret knowledge we have held for thousands of years. His name is Kra. He already has very great power, which he can use to heal or harm. He can make powerful medicine - and powerful poison. He can also control the weather in the sacred mountains, but this is actually not so special. Many human shamans from this land have been able to do this for centuries. He wants much more. He knows that we guard the greatest, most precious treasure on Earth. He plans to steal the sacred Stones and sell them at great price to scientists from the West. He craves wealth, and the power wealth confers more than anything."

"You already know that the stones you have seen are not just beautiful trinkets. Below our cave, deep under the Himalaya, are many, many more. Much deeper under the surface, *there is one stone which will enable us to travel vast distances through space in no time at all.* Our ancestors believed there were even stones below that with the power to create new life. All this Kra will take, if he can, but I must tell you, Ingrid, the more power humans have, the more they will use it for evil purposes. This is the human way. Power does not liberate you, it enslaves you."

Suddenly Mamo's face changed as she seemed to see something or someone behind Ingrid. She was enraged. She let go of Ingrid's hand and stood to her full terrifying height – at least eight feet tall – looking ahead of her, snarling, revealing all her huge, yellow teeth. Ingrid turned, cowering, to look in the same direction, clutching the purple stone, which until that moment she had forgotten. Red and yellow lights seemed to be flickering all around, but she could see no-one. The flickering lights became wilder and more rapid making Ingrid feel dizzy.

"What is it, Mamo?" she shouted, "What can you see? What is it? *What is it?*"

Ingrid woke up; still calling something…was it "Mamo" or "Mother"? She looked across to her parents, who were snoring lightly. Her mother turned over, muttering. Ingrid tried to recall the whole dream, and to remember all Mamo's words, but they were fading, and she was so tired…

As she felt herself drifting back, she tried to return to the dream, to recapture the image of Mamo's face. The image of a face was now coming towards her. It was hurtling towards her as though it was about to smash into her. This was not Mamo.

Coming straight at her were a pair of glaring red eyes, a foul, gaping mouth, a head crowned with a garland of tiny, shrivelled skulls. The repulsive mouth gaped wider as though about to swallow her. It roared and swerved away at the last moment to be replaced by another face speeding towards her from the pit of hell. She tried to scream but no sound would emerge. This face was flaming red, and the teeth in its mouth were all sharpened to points. A snake's tongue flickered in and out of the disgusting, stinking mouth. This face was also crowned with tiny skulls like the one before. It laughed in delight at her terror. It came so close that the tongue momentarily brushed her face. She felt revolting wetness drip onto her cheek. She strained her whole body in an attempt to scream or move, but the monstrous creatures seemed to have paralysed her, just as some snakes do, before devouring their prey.

Despite her horror and revulsion, she had an idea in the still rational part of her head, telling her she had seen these faces before. She felt she could liberate herself *if only she could remember.* The vicious, snarling, laughing faces continued to whirl around her, as Ingrid strained to move.

On and on, round and – yes! That was it! She had seen them around the circumference of the mandala in the Buddhist monastery they had stayed in overnight on their journey. They were just scary images of wrathful gods – just pictures on a wall-hanging – what had they called it? A thangka, or something. As her dreaming mind focussed on a real memory, so the creatures vanished instantaneously, and she was in her beautiful, blissful bed at home, *so* comfortable, *so* safe.

Her brain dragged itself back to consciousness and the reality of her lumpy sleeping bag and the cold Himalayan night. She had been crying in her sleep and there were wet patches on the pillow of her sleeping bag. She did not care. She was awake and alive.

Her head found a dry place on the pillow and she fell into a profound, dreamless sleep.

* * *

The Stones and the Shaman

When Ingrid awoke, her parents had already been up for some time and were preparing with Pasang and Pemba for the day's search. As she emerged from the tent, Tshering saw her and immediately gestured to the breakfast food which he had been starting to clear away: millet porridge, naan bread, hard-boiled eggs and goat's cheese. He also poured some tea from the saucepan, which had been boiling furiously over the fire, into a cup for her. She thanked him and took the cup. He nodded and returned to his clearing up.

As she sat on one of the yak-wool blankets near the low table, and sipped the slightly cheesy tea, she realised that her headache from the day before had gone. Her eyes felt heavy and swollen from crying, but she felt well. She quietly helped herself to porridge, and watched the boys, twenty yards or so from her, preparing one of the yaks for the day's journey. They were working in silence. Apart from the odd yak grunt and distant vulture cries, all was peaceful. She stared across in wonder at the beauty of Everest in the middle distance before her, still hazy in the morning light.

She thought about the night's dreams. They had felt so real. Suddenly it occurred to her that yesterday's whole meeting with the yeti could have been a dream. She had after all been suffering from a little altitude sickness, as well as exhaustion. Perhaps she had just been fast asleep on the hillside all afternoon and had only been woken by the goat chewing her rucksack.

Almost before that thought was completed, she recalled her one piece of irrefutable evidence. She put down her porridge bowl and spoon and reached into her pocket. Before she could pull the stone out, she became aware that Sonam was approaching her. He spoke quickly and quietly in impeccable English,

"Miss Ingrid, please be careful. Please do not..." he searched for the correct word, "involve yourself with Kra."

CHAPTER FIVE
The Quest

The name sent a shock wave through her brain. She grabbed Sonam's arm,

"I didn't know you could speak English! What do you know about Kra? Please tell me."

"He is dangerous. You must keep away."

Sonam's deep brown eyes looked directly into Ingrid's vivid green ones, imploring and fearful.

"Sonam!"

Pasang was calling. Sonam pulled away from Ingrid, and walked over to help Pasang, who immediately began talking to him very fast with much gesticulation. Ingrid's parents were almost ready to set off, and her father was approaching. She set her face into a bland expression.

"Ingrid, we are heading West today and expect to be gone for at least four, possibly five hours. Tshering will prepare some lunch for you. The boys will be leaving us for a few days to collect the other yaks that we'll need for the onward trip to Kanchenjunga. Pemba and Pasang will be coming with your mother and me. Your mother and I suggest you stay near the camp today as you are obviously tired. You can go off and do some sketching, but please stay within sight of the camp. If you see any interesting plants and wish to practise your botanical illustration, so much the better."

"Thank you, Daddy. Good luck. I hope you have some good finds," said Ingrid, reaching up to kiss him, "Don't worry about me. I'll be perfectly fine."

Her mother rushed over, "Goodbye, darling. Please be good and stay near the camp today, won't you? Don't forget to have a go with your new Brownie camera – I've unpacked it for you - but don't waste the film!" she said, hugging her daughter, "And have a rest in the tent after lunch."

"I will, Mother, don't worry," said Ingrid, "Have a good day."

As her parents departed, Ingrid turned round to look for Sonam. He was already descending in the direction of the present home of the yak-herders, several miles away, with Ketsun. They wore thin plimsolls and rushed along the rocky terrain as nimbly as goats. She stared at his back, willing him to turn around and look at her. She could almost imagine that he was aware of her look. He did not turn back. They were soon out of sight.

Ingrid grabbed some bread and cheese from the breakfast table, wrapping it in some of the waxed paper of which they seemed to have inexhaustible supplies; collected her sketching materials from the tent, and put them all in her rucksack. She decided against taking her precious new camera in case it got damaged. She could just imagine Ketu finding it and smashing it to bits.

Looking back to make sure Tshering was too busy to notice her, she set off for the yeti cave. She made herself walk at a steady pace, suppressing a sense of dread which kept threatening to overwhelm her. From time to time, she touched the stone in her pocket, and tried not to think about her "destiny". It was Sonam's words that were making her burn with curiosity, yet it was Sonam's words that made her feel such dread. Contrary to all common sense and reason, she had to go back to the cave. She concentrated on the route.

When she was finally in sight of the entrance to the yeti cave, she saw movement in the dense scrub in front of it, and Kol-pa and Ketu emerged; Ketu jumping up and down in excitement. Ingrid suddenly felt shy. She just said, "Hi!" and gave them an awkward wave. Kol-pa beckoned her across, and helped her through the prickly branches.

"Ingrid, we knew you would return," said Kol-pa, grinning her yellow-toothed grin, as they entered the sweet-smelling, brightly lit cave, "Today you will see the things which Kra covets. You will come with us through the deep tunnels into the caves at the heart of the Himalaya. No human has ever been where we will take you today. You will be the only one. You will fulfil the Prophecy. Will you come?"

Ingrid peeled off her rucksack, and took Kol-pa's hand.

"Listen, Kol-pa, I have to tell you something. Of course I want to see your treasures, but I am not brave. I'm just not. You need to know that. I don't know why you think I can help you, or what this Prophecy is all about, but I'm here, so – yes, I'll come."

As they walked with echoing steps through the rooms of Kol-pa's home, with Ketu bouncing around them, Mamo appeared from a room off to the right, with another female yeti, as big as herself but evidently younger.

"Ingrid, my dear child, thank you for returning," said Mamo, bending forward and placing her huge hand on Ingrid's head, with extreme fondness, "I would like you to meet Nyima, my daughter; the mother of Kol-pa and Ketu."

The younger yeti was very beautiful in a solemn, yeti-ish way. She, too, wore a Speaking Stone pendant around her neck. She spoke to Ingrid,

"Ingrid, the task you are about to undertake requires more gratitude from us than it is possible to measure. The meh-teh are now not so many. We will not be here for much longer. In the future, you will tell the world about us, and of the things you have seen. With all my heart, thank you."

"But I thought I was just going down to see the rest of the caves, and the other stones – I don't know about a task. What *is* the task?"

There were fleeting glances between the elder yeti, and Ingrid thought she saw Mamo frown at Nyima, who replied,

"It is just our way of speaking, Ingrid. I mean, of course, the task of your journey to the deep tunnels. You are indeed going to see the rest of the Stones, and Kol-pa will look after you on the descent. Do not worry."

"Well, I do want to help you and I will do my best, but I don't know if there's much I can do."

"You will see, my dear," said Mamo, "go now with the children and they will show you. Take care – the path is not easy for human feet."

"Come on! Come on!" screeched Ketu, pulling at Ingrid's jacket, "I know the way!"

Kol-pa took Ingrid's arm and guided her to an opening to a much darker cave. They were followed by the two adult females. Nyima handed Kol-pa a seed-pod flask strung with heavy twine, which Kol-pa slung over her shoulder. She took some other objects from an alcove in the wall near the opening,

"Here you are, children, wear these Light Stones around your necks. They will shine enough to show you the way," said Nyima, taking three necklaces from a woven basket near the entrance, and placing one over each head.

Ingrid looked down at the beautiful object. On a string of thin twine hung a gleaming pendant which glowed softly, greenish white. It was cool and smooth to touch. She looked up to say thank you, but the faces of the yeti suddenly appeared so sinister in the eerie green light that a surge of fear welled up inside her, and no sound emerged from her throat.

For a moment, the two hideous faces from her dream flashed through her mind, and every nerve in her body seemed to cry out,

"Don't do this! Go home!"

She reached into her pocket and touched the purple stone, feeling her panic ease a little as she did so.

"Go now, children," whispered Mamo, and with no further word, Kol-pa and Ketu guided Ingrid into the cave.

* * *

What seemed at first a cave rapidly became little more than a narrow tunnel, with steps that descended sharply. They had to go in single file: Kol-pa, Ingrid, then Ketu, who had desisted from all bouncing and jumping as soon as they entered. They were all subdued.

The horror of the mandala faces remained with Ingrid, leaving her with a vestige of unease that would not go away. Also, she was not happy to be in an extremely confined space, which was steadily becoming smaller. Before her, Kol-pa had to stoop double as she continued down. The walls were smooth and damp. There was nothing to hold on to.

Suddenly, something scuttled over Ingrid's foot. She yelled out in horror. Looking down, she discovered hundreds of small, pale creatures rushing in a purposeful way across the floor of the tunnel. She could not see well enough to identify them – spiders?...beetles?...scorpions?

The Stones and the Shaman

After a sharp, "Sssshhhhh!" from Kol-pa, Ingrid choked back any further screams. She could hear Ketu behind her, kicking the creatures out of the way.

"What *are* those things?" whispered Ingrid crossly.

"Oh, we call them stonestalkers – the bigger ones are venomous, but these tiny ones can't hurt you," replied Kol-pa, breezily, "but whatever happens, please try not to scream!"

"Anyway," piped up Ketu, still scattering the stonestalkers with deft swipes of his feet, "how could they sting you through those silly great boots you wear?"

Ingrid spun round to glare at the smaller yeti,

"Well, if I can't be stung, then the boots aren't so silly, are they?" she said crossly.

Kol-pa answered Ketu without turning round,

"No need to be rude, Ketu. Humans only have delicate, thin skin on their feet and need such coverings."

Ingrid felt too angry and frightened to say anything. This tedious, hot, cramped trudging was dampening her curiosity until she felt she had no great interest in these "Stones of Power" anyway. Her only comfort was the pale green stone, hanging from her neck. At least it had no batteries to fail in this dark, claustrophobic place.

They soon passed the stonestalkers and their purposeful marching. After perhaps half an hour of rhythmic downward stepping, the gradient began to seem less steep. To her great relief, their way was now lit not only by their Light Stones, but by a rich deep violet glow, coming from a new cave ahead of them. As they entered, the sight which met her eyes took her breath away.

CHAPTER SIX
Hearing and Seeing

This vast cave pulsated with colour. Of course, Ingrid had seen precious stones before. Her mother had a sapphire in her engagement ring, and other exquisite jewellery, mostly inherited, including a gorgeous lapis lazuli necklace. Ingrid herself had been given a very old amethyst necklace from a great aunt. All those blues and violets paled pathetically, like cheap trinkets, against the stone now before her. The strata in this rock face, blue, purple, violet, had light – life – and even, Ingrid somehow sensed, *awareness.*

As she stared at the central stratum, a deep purple from which the Speaking Stones were obviously mined, Ingrid began to feel mesmerised. Her head was filling up with a Babel of whispering words until they all seemed to slot into place and she felt a surge of astonishing power: she could think a thought in Spanish, Swedish or Swahili; she could think in yeti, gorilla or marmoset. She felt her head would burst with the feast of new vocabulary and syntax being swallowed up by her brain. She held her head in her hands, but continued to stare.

She laughed with sheer incredulity at what was happening to her. She realised the two yeti were looking at her, smiling their comically wide, toothy smiles. Ketu burst into his chimpanzee laughter.

"It's a good feeling, isn't it?" laughed Kol-pa.

"Good?" replied Ingrid, "it's the best feeling in the world."

"I know – it's wonderful. It makes you feel that we're all the same. But we must move on down now as swiftly as we can. Let's go."

The smooth blue-streaked floor would have been impossible to walk on, but there was a path along which the surface had been somehow roughened. They walked across this path to the opening of another tunnel, dodging stalactites as they went.

As they walked, Ingrid asked,

"Kol-pa, what's the hurry? Why is there little time?"

Before Kol-pa could answer, there was a deafening rumbling sound – unmistakably a major rock-fall somewhere within the caves. The ground beneath them shook, and several rocks, some as big as a yeti's head, fell from the walls, landing only a foot or so from them. Ingrid stopped and grasped Kol-pa's arm in terror. Ketu whimpered, and clung on to his sister.

"What on earth is happening? Are we going to be trapped? Oh, please, *please* let's go back now – while we still can," begged Ingrid in sheer panic.

"*No*. We will not be trapped, and we cannot yet go back. Kra is trying to frighten us. He has the power to do these things. We must continue down. We need the red stone, Ingrid," Kol-pa hesitated, "Only you can get it for us."

"D'you mean Kra is down here somewhere now? For God's sake, we must go!" Ingrid was yelling at Kol-pa in desperation.

Kol-pa said nothing, but put her arm round Ingrid firmly, taking her forward to the next tunnel. The sounds of falling rocks subsided. The silence and darkness of the new tunnel was sinister, as though something horrifying was waiting for them, somewhere inside.

At that moment Ingrid felt completely drained. Having experienced the full force of the Speaking Stone, her mind felt weakened; her body limp. She felt she had no vestige of courage or strength left in her. She spoke softly and slowly,

Hearing and Seeing

"Kol-pa, listen. I feel very, very frightened. I don't think I can carry on. I thought you just wanted to show me what was down here, just to admire some sort of treasure trove, but all this stuff with Kra and rock-falls and stones that do crazy things to your mind…it's all too much. This task – getting this red stone for you - I don't know why you need me to do it, but I'm sorry I just can't do this. I'm just an ordinary eleven year old girl from Cornwall, not some questing heroine. Please, please, take me back," pleaded Ingrid, her last words, "take me back" echoing down the tunnel.

Kol-pa looked into Ingrid's eyes.

"Ingrid, if you do not do this, the meh-teh will die."

Ketu's huge liquid eyes were staring up at Ingrid. The two yeti waited as Ingrid struggled with her fear.

"Come on, then," she said, "let's go."

* * *

The next tunnel was far worse than the previous one. It was hot, cramped, steep, and had many loose stones so that Ingrid was soon bruised and grazed from falls along the way.

By the light of her stone pendant, she could just make out the time on her watch. It was almost two hours since she had left the camp and she had been in the caves for over an hour of that time. She had no idea how long it was going to take to arrive at their destination, but in all probability, she would not be back before her parents' return. No doubt, her father would be too engrossed in his work to notice her absence, but her mother would certainly notice, especially after yesterday. Ingrid would be in serious trouble. With disturbing feelings of guilt, she realised that Tshering would be in trouble, too, for failing to keep an eye on her.

There was nothing she could do. She just had to keep going. Suddenly, Ketu was babbling in front of her,

"Look, Ingrid – the green cave! Do you like the green cave?"

There were no shades of green anywhere above ground to compare with the strata in the vast cave they now entered. Kol-pa snapped at Ketu,

"Yes, alright, Ketu. We mustn't linger in here, remember?" she turned to Ingrid, holding her firmly by the arm, "Come on, Ingrid, this is not a good place for you to be, we must move on as quickly as we can."

"But it's *so* beautiful, I just need to stop and take it all in," replied Ingrid, mesmerised.

At the highest point, and running through the roof of the cave, the strata were palest green and luminous like their Light Stone pendants. This made the cave cheerfully bright. Ingrid enjoyed the welcome relief of so much brilliant light and was reluctant to move from it. Through the central part of the cave, the greens graded down to a clear, true green which glittered in a way that Ingrid found hypnotic. This rock seemed like the stuff of deep magic.

"Ingrid, no, we *must* move on," said Kol-pa urgently as she dragged Ingrid forward, "Ketu, pick up some pieces of Healing Stone from the floor while we're here," then speaking again to Ingrid, "Ingrid, we really need to go now. Don't make me carry you out."

Ingrid was vaguely aware of Ketu scrabbling around, collecting shards of the dark green stone which littered the floor, when suddenly a vision flashed before her eyes: Sonam's face was staring back at her, shocked and full of concern. It was as though he was there in front of her. He made a silent gesture to her that she did not understand, and then he was gone. Ketu leapt up from the floor as a hissing sound began to echo round the cave.

"Sorry, Ingrid, it's time to *go*," said Kol-pa, now lifting Ingrid bodily and jogging between stalagmites and stalactites to reach the next tunnel, "Ketu, *run.*"

All around the cave, bright green snakes were slithering out of crevices in the central strata of rock, moving with appalling speed down the walls, onto the floor and towards the three children. The snakes had dazzling amber eyes which gleamed dangerously as they caught the light. Their tongues flickered constantly. As they approached her feet, Kol-pa's jog broke into a run. Ingrid, now startled out of her hypnotic state, was screaming.

"Shut up, Ingrid, please!" panted Kol-pa, "they'll be infuriated by your noise – you're just making things worse, just *shut up!*"

The moment they were out of the green cave, all hissing stopped as though the snakes had instantly lost interest. Kol-pa put Ingrid down.

"I did tell you it wasn't a good place to stay," smiled Kol-pa calmly as she caught her breath.

"Well, *thanks very much,* maybe you should have told me first?" said Ingrid sarcastically.

Kol-pa just laughed, as they continued along the new tunnel, "I didn't want to frighten you!" and she turned to Ketu, "Ketu, give Ingrid some pieces of the Healing Stone please."

Ketu did as he was told and Ingrid found she knew what to do. She placed the hand holding the stones against her chest and breathed deeply. She felt healed and comforted as Kol-pa began to explain,

"The rock you saw in the centre of the cave can only be safely used by the Wise Ones. Centuries ago, snakes' eggs were placed inside the walls as a deterrent to the uninitiated. As you see, they have thrived! It's for our own good, you see, because the green stone which we call the Telling Stone can show the Wise Ones the future. If you are not trained to do this, it is very, very dangerous. But it is also very tempting. It can damage your mind. It is safer to be frightened off by snakes than to linger in that cave."

"But how do you take the Light Stones and the Healing Stones out of there?" asked Ingrid as they plodded along.

"Only the initiated go there to mine the stones we need, including the Telling Stone. They can calm the snakes and take only what is needed. Mamo is our Wise One and she has some Telling Stone. By the way," she added, "keep the Healing Stones in your pocket. They may prove useful later."

Ingrid did so.

"One more question! What on earth do those snakes find to eat?"

"Oh, small stonestalkers, mostly, and also the tiny cave spiders that live down here. The snakes' venom is deadly, in case you were wondering, but they wouldn't be much of a deterrent otherwise, would they?" she chuckled.

Ingrid did not know whether to believe her, but she did not comment. She walked on quietly, puzzling over her vision of Sonam.

CHAPTER SEVEN
Heat, Steam and Speed

As they walked ever downward, it occurred to Ingrid that conditions were becoming increasingly hot and damp. Wasn't it normally cooler below the earth? She was not sure – she had never really studied geology, or anything much else that was scientific, apart from plants. Something didn't feel right about this oppressive, sticky heat, though.

Suddenly, Kol-pa stopped. Ingrid could hear the sound of bubbling water. By the dim green light of their pendants, she could see the concern on the faces of the two yeti as they exchanged glances. Ketu whimpered nervously.

"Ingrid, the path in the cave we are about to enter is a narrow ledge," whispered Kol-pa, "There will be a smooth wall on our right. To our left, the shelf falls steeply down to a huge underground lake. The water in the lake is very, very hot. Boiling. We will walk slowly, holding hands, and it would be better for you if you close your eyes. It is not too far before we come to the next tunnel. Are you ready?"

Although she felt sick with fear, Ingrid felt there was no choice, and was about to say so when Ketu began whispering to Kol-pa. Kol-pa looked uncertain and troubled. She began again,

"Wait. There is something else. There are creatures in the water. Ketu is right – I must tell you this before we go on. You must be *completely quiet.* These creatures are what the humans of these lands call dragons. I know that you people from the West do not believe in them. Let me tell you, dragons are real, but they do not eat humans or meh-teh, only the strange, spiny fish that live in these boiling waters. Also, they are nearly blind. Nevertheless, if they hear us, they will feel threatened and will attack us to protect themselves. They can fly fast and their steaming breath alone is enough to kill us. If their bodies were to come too near, their scalding heat would flay us alive," she paused and looked hard into Ingrid's eyes, "Have I told you enough to make you move as silently as the meh-teh?"

Nauseous and trembling, Ingrid nodded.

"Close your eyes and hold our hands. Concentrate on being silent. Let's go."

The very thought of trying to be silent made Ingrid's breath come fast and loud. She remembered the stones, and plunged her hand into her pocket for just a moment to hold them before proceeding. She then took a deep breath and finally grasped the outstretched hands of the waiting yeti children. They inched slowly forward. Ingrid could feel her back against the smooth wall. Kol-pa was in front of her, holding her right hand, Ketu behind, holding her left. She could hear constant bubbling and loud sighing breathing from far below. She was dripping with sweat, still wearing all the layers of clothing she had put on in the morning. There were occasional sudden splashes of water and snuffling, grunting sounds. Her legs were wobbling so much she knew she would fall if she let go of her friends for a second. Yet despite her fear she had a crazy urge to look to see what was causing the noise. She resisted the temptation and kept her eyes closed tightly. She dreaded to imagine the vastness of the drop down to the lake, yet on the other hand, no distance could be great enough to separate her from those fearful creatures.

Suddenly, the path appeared to have a sharp downward gradient which Ingrid had not expected. She let out a tiny involuntary scream as she slipped slightly, falling against Kol-pa. That scream was enough. All the grunting, snuffling and splashing below stopped. Kol-pa stopped in her tracks. There was the intense, strained silence of creatures down below, waiting, listening. Then, Ingrid's terror went off the scale as Kol-pa yelled,

"GO!"

Heat , Steam and Speed

She hardly knew what was happening any more as she found herself being dragged and shoved by Kol-pa and Ketu who were bounding for their lives along the steep, narrow, slippery path. Eyes now wide open; Ingrid could see a small tunnel entrance not far away. The heat was intensifying unbearably and she could hear hideous screeching sounds as the dragons flew upwards towards them. The beating of their wings was so fast and powerful that it made an unearthly rhythmic howling as loud as their screaming cries. Ingrid herself was screaming and Ketu, frightened out of his wits, was shrieking chimp-like alarm calls at the top of his voice. Kol-pa was now pushing herself frantically through the tunnel entrance, never letting go of Ingrid's hand. Ketu pushed Ingrid through with tremendous force and just had time to squeeze through himself as Kol-pa heaved a rock in front of the opening to block out the dragons' searing heat. They heard frightful crashes against the rock as the dragons hurled themselves, seconds too late, at their intruders.

The new tunnel seemed cool by comparison with the boiling hell they had just left. Gradually the terrifying crashes subsided as the dragons gave up the chase and returned to the lake. All three sat exhausted, heads on knees. Ingrid was sobbing helplessly. Ketu was whimpering like a baby. Kol-pa was silent.

The moment before Ingrid had been shoved into the tunnel, she had looked back to see the dragons: countless numbers of them, ranging in size from about six to twelve feet in length. Their bodies glistened like eels or worms, the smaller ones pinkish-red in colour, the larger ones red-brown. Their wings reminded Ingrid of pictures she had seen of pterodactyls – more like webbed arms than wings - and as they flew so much steam rose from their bodies that they created a thick scalding cloud above themselves. But in that moment, it was the sight of their faces that would remain imprinted on Ingrid's mind forever. Their pink skin was wrinkled, their eyes closed like new-born kittens; their beak-like mouths gaped wide showing double rows of razor-sharp teeth and flickering, steaming forked tongues; their nostrils flared as they smelled out their enemies.

As she sat, crying, Ingrid's fear was rapidly mutating into a rage which finally burst out of her in a torrent of words whispered through her tears,

"I nearly *died* in there! Do you realise nobody would ever have known what happened to me? What on earth did you think you were doing, leading me into a place like that? What are you really up to? What *is* this all about? I thought you were my *friends*, but you're not, you're just ignorant, idiotic, pea-brained…*monkeys!*"

Ketu stared at Ingrid in horror, but Kol-pa remained motionless and the expression on her face revealed nothing. After several seconds, she spoke, calmly,

"If I were as much like a monkey as *your* species, I would take Ketu with me and leave you right here, right now. Fortunately for you, we have more civilised values. And in case you had forgotten, it was your noise that disturbed the dragons, and we actually saved your life."

Ingrid now cringed with embarrassment at the stupidity and rudeness of her insult. Kol-pa's words were like a cold shower bringing her to her senses.

"You're right – that was unforgivably rude. I am so sorry," she replied, looking everywhere but at Kol-pa, "May I ask you a question, please?"

"Of course," answered Kol-pa coolly.

"When I have collected this red stone – whatever it is – for you, do we have to…go back the way we came?"

CHAPTER EIGHT
Voices

"I don't know," replied Kol-pa simply, "I've never been this far before."

"You've never been in that place before! And you've never seen the dragons?"

"Oh yes, I've seen the dragons," said Kol-pa, nodding and smiling a little. She appeared to have forgiven Ingrid already, but the cold look on her face a few seconds before was still on Ingrid's mind.

"I've seen the dragons, Ingrid, I've seen the dragons," Ketu butted in, gently shaking Ingrid's arm to gain her attention.

"Yes, alright, Ketu, don't interrupt, please. As I was saying," continued Kol-pa, "sometimes they come higher up the tunnels if they get lost searching for new hot springs, especially in years when they've had a lot of young and the lake is getting over-crowded. They can't stray far from the heat and moisture, though, or they quickly cool and die. They live for a very long time – perhaps two hundred years or more – but when their time has come, they fly up out of the caves to die on the mountain tops. The cool, dry air finishes them off very quickly, and then their bodies are consumed by vultures. The humans around here grind up their bones to make medicine."

"But in answer to your first question, no, I have never been to the Dragon Cave before. Mamo told me the way to come, and I don't know if there is any other way back."

"Oh well, then," said Ingrid wearily, "you'd better take me to this stone you want me to collect, so we can get it over and done with. There's no choice but to keep going, is there?"

She peeled off her jacket and flung it on to the floor beside her. Ketu cuddled her and stroked her damp hair, saying quietly,

"Ketu is Ingrid's friend. Always."

"I know, Ketu, I know. Friends always."

She hugged him back, tightly. Kol-pa, who was now standing a little apart, clearly ready to move on, moved back towards Ingrid and placed her enormous hand gently on the girl's shoulder. The two yeti helped her to stand up.

Once more Ingrid found herself slipping, sliding and occasionally crawling along yet another hot, cramped rocky tunnel. As they progressed, it gradually seemed less dark, even though they were descending sharply. Their green pendants were no longer their only light-source: there was a red glow coming from the walls of the tunnel itself. It could have been some new energy coming from the rock, or possibly the knowledge that the end of her journey was approaching, but Ingrid found herself feeling strangely light-hearted and care-free. The descent quite abruptly flattened out and their progress became easy. The tunnel was now high enough for all of them to stand upright. To her joy, Ingrid could even stretch her arms up to relieve the dull ache in her back. The red glow was so powerful that the yeti's blond hair now looked deep pink.

"It's here," said Kol-pa suddenly, "just round this bend. "Ingrid, take off your pendant and give it to me – you don't need it here – and take off this wool covering thing." (She meant Ingrid's jumper), "You must make yourself as small as possible."

In her calm, relaxed mood, Ingrid did as she was told, dropping her jumper onto the ground, and awaited her instructions. They rounded the bend together and Kol-pa continued, her face looking eerie in the strange red light,

"You see before you the place where there was a rock-fall many years ago, when Mamo's own grandmother was no older that I am now. Since that time none of the meh-teh has been farther than where we now stand. There is a room beyond the boulders you see. For thousands of years that room was a sacred place for us. It was once a rite of passage for every young meh-teh to pass through the Dragon Cave alone and to enter the Sacred Room. They would then perform a series of secret rituals decided by the Matriarch of the time before returning as an adult member of the group."

"In the centre of the room is a table. On the table is a carved stone box. In the box is the stone we must have. The Universe Stone. You must enter the room, open the box and take the stone. *Try not to look at the stone any longer than you have to.* Place it in this pouch as quickly as you can," she handed Ingrid a small goatskin bag as she said this, "and put it in your pocket so that your hands are free to climb out. You must come out as quickly as you can. Now, you are going to enter the room by climbing up to the top of these rocks – the energy within the rocks will help you – and you will find a small gap at the top. It should be just big enough for you to squeeze through so that you can climb down the other side and into the room. While you are in there, Ketu and I will go and look for another way out of the caves. Do you understand all I have said?"

"Yes, that's fine. I understand," said Ingrid easily. She felt as though she were in a dream, in which anything was possible.

In fact, the gap was so small that Ingrid would never normally have considered trying to enter it. The pile of rocks looked steep and unstable.

"Here, have some water before you go," said Kol-pa, passing her the flask. Ingrid gulped the water down greedily, suddenly realising how desperately thirsty she was. She gave the flask back to Kol-pa and turned to the rock-pile.

"Alright, I'm ready," she said. Both yeti hugged her and then she began her climb.

Having been on several Alpine expeditions with her parents, Ingrid was not at all bad at scrambling over rocky terrain. She clambered over the unstable rocks with unnatural confidence. It felt easy.

When she was half-way up, she turned around to wave at Kol-pa and Ketu, but there was no sign of them. For a fleeting moment, an ice-cold shudder of fear ran through her. Then she remembered that, of course, they were just looking for another way out. Nevertheless, at that moment a little of her confidence seemed to drain away. She turned back to face the rock to find her next hand-hold. She remained motionless for half a minute, breathing deeply and trying to compose herself. She was just about to continue when she thought she heard quiet laughter a short distance behind her. It was a human laugh, mean and cruel. She heard a voice in slightly accented English whisper,

"All alone, now, Ingrid?"

She looked frantically around her. There was no-one there. Her mind must be playing tricks. She focussed on the rocks. She had to continue. All at once, the rocks in front of her face were transforming themselves into the flaming red mandala faces of her dreams, laughing at her and revealing their needle-sharp teeth and hideous forked tongues. Every rock before her was a different demon face, laughing and mocking. She could not move. There was tormenting laughter all around her. She closed her eyes as tightly as she could and screamed.

"Ingrid! Ingrid!" the evil voice was calling in a sing-song voice, "Your so-called friends are never coming back for you, you know. You see, they don't really like humans. They don't like you, and they don't like me. You've been tricked. If you go into that room you will never get out. You will die there, Ingrid, you will die!"

The word "die" was echoing all around her. For a moment she opened her eyes and the rocks were just rocks again. Silence returned. It would be easy to climb back down. But then, what? Go through the Dragon Cave again? Alone? Even if she made it through that far, there were endless tunnel entrances; she could never find her way back. She looked around again to look for the source of the voice. There was nothing in the tunnel but glowing red emptiness. She could not go forward. She could not go back.

Then, just by her ear, in a harsh, hissing whisper, the voice came again,

"It doesn't have to end like this, Ingrid. *We could help each other.*"

She could almost feel the hot breath from the voice on her neck. She shook her head rapidly from side to side as though she could rid herself of the voice that way. Again, the harsh, insistent whisper,

"We have so much in common. If you *help* me, I could get you out of here."

This is *not real*, this is *not happening*, Ingrid repeated to herself, and then she shouted in desperation,

"Why don't you show yourself?"

The response was just that cruel, mocking laughter again. Ingrid yelled,

"Go away! I'm imagining you. You are NOT REAL. Go away!"

Suddenly, she could hear the padding of yeti feet running fast from another tunnel.

"Ingrid," called Kol-pa in an urgent whisper, "Stop shouting! You'll cause a rock-fall! What's the matter?"

Ketu was jumping up and down, making loud shushing noises, a finger to his lips.

"And you be quiet, too, Ketu!" said Kol-pa, "Ingrid, tell us what happened."

"A man's voice was in here – telling me not to go on. He said you – oh, never mind. Listen. The rocks were *alive*…I can't explain. It must have been *him* - Kra, I mean…I was terrified, it was a nightmare. Look, please, just stay with me, *please.*"

"I feel his presence," replied Kol-pa grimly. "Ingrid, we will not move. We will stay here for you. You must go into the room now. It will be fine, but you must go *now.*"

Kol-pa no longer looked like a six-year-old primate, but like a wise and very old woman. There was no arguing with her. Ingrid went. The rocks remained simply rocks for the short duration of Ingrid's scramble to the top. The gap at the top looked even smaller once she was level with it, and she could see that she would have to crawl about three yards to get into the room itself. The rocks were throbbing with light. In the room, there appeared to be an ever changing spectrum of colour, as though there was some kind of living, intelligent presence in there. She took a deep breath, exhaled, and went through.

CHAPTER NINE
To Take the Stone

Ingrid squeezed through the glowing, pulsating tunnel by force of will. The shimmering, spinning lights before her made her feel so confused, she hardly knew which way was up. Then, as her head finally emerged into the space beyond, the moving lights came to a halt.

She was now desperate to escape from her confinement and struggle down the rocks any way she could. Head and arms first, like a baby from the womb; Ingrid launched herself in a frantic scramble downwards on to the floor of the room, about twelve feet below. Her arrival on to the smooth floor was somehow by a forward roll, finally landing flat on her back. She had banged her head quite hard on the way, but it did not seem to bother her.

Her body lay motionless as her eyes scanned the room. Slowly, she raised herself up onto her elbows to take a better look. The room was an enormous dome, the perfection of its shape marred only by the heap of marbled crimson and scarlet rocks down which she had just scrambled and rolled. There were elaborate carvings above the rock heap showing where the arched doorway to the room had been. The rest of the room, which was light as day, was decorated by an exquisite mural depicting the solar system and innumerable other similar systems. Each group of planets had a different coloured central star, ranging through the first part of the spectrum: red, orange or yellow.

Ingrid felt peaceful and happy, marvelling at the beautiful and loving workmanship (work-yeti-ship, she supposed) that had created the scene before her. She felt she could stay there forever. It seemed even a happy idea that she might give up all this effort and struggle and simply die, just where she was.

Slowly, a small niggling thought began to buzz vaguely around her brain. She had a foggy memory of coming to this place for a reason. An important reason. What was it? Really, she could hardly be bothered to think about it. She wanted to rest there and absorb all the beauty. She continued to gaze about. Before her, was a long, heavy table constructed from the red rock. It resembled an altar. On the altar was a box. *The box!* With a jolt, the fog in her brain cleared. She knew why she was there. With a panicky fear that she was losing her mind, Ingrid leapt to her feet. All she had to do was complete the simple task. Open the carved box. Take the stone. Leave the room.

She walked unsteadily towards the table. Her head now ached painfully. She was beginning to hear a humming sound, but could not be sure whether it was coming from inside or outside her own head. The box had begun to glow. Then she realised. The lights she had seen earlier had been coming from the box itself, and they were beginning to dance again. The closer she came, the faster and more dazzling was the light display. It was like the aurora borealis she had once seen in the Highlands of Scotland, but infinitely more spectacular. The light seemed to be intelligent, dancing for her enjoyment. As she now stood at the table directly in front of the box, the lights filled the whole room and once again, Ingrid had the bizarre feeling that it would be fine to die, right here, right now. If she just stayed where she was, looking at the most beautiful thing any human being would ever see. But…there was a tiny pathway in her brain sending an ancient memory about a job to do…Open the carved box. Take the stone. Leave the room.

At that moment, a voice of pure evil whispered in her ear,

"You will die here, Ingrid, you will die!"

The voice filled her with such terror that her mind jolted back to the task. She grabbed at the box, and then screamed with pain, drawing back her hand, clutching it to her body with her other arm. She could not even tell whether her hand had been subjected to intense heat or intense cold, but the searing pain was extreme. She felt angry, desperate, hopeless. Insanely, she grabbed at the box again. The same pain tore into her hand. She wrenched it away. The lights were now whirling with such speed and ferocity she could barely even see the box. The humming was deafening. Her head was swimming. What was she to do? Then as she stared into the light, all hope abandoned, the lid slowly opened of its own accord. As it did so, the lights gradually slowed down, the swirling spectrum diminished, losing first its violet, indigo and blue, then its range of greens, its yellow and orange, until nothing was left but pure red light. She reached inside. A smooth, cool ovoid shape met her grasp, and her hand immediately closed over it. In the seconds before she took it from the box, some other important memory was reaching out to her, but it would not unfurl. She had the stone in her closed fist. It only remained to leave the room.

She stepped back from the table. The lid of the box slowly closed. No light or sound came from it now. The only light in the room was coming from her fist. Slowly she uncurled her fingers to look at the thing she had struggled so far to collect. As each finger opened, more and more red light flooded into the room. By the time Ingrid's hand was completely open, and the stone revealed in all its terrifying beauty, nothing else was visible in the room: only pure red light. At the same moment, two things happened. Ingrid felt herself being pulled and spun into some kind of vortex: at the same time a distant voice was yelling,

"Close your hand NOW! Put the stone in the bag!"

CHAPTER TEN
Kra

Even today, in Ingrid's old age, she looks back to that moment and wonders what made her obey that distant voice, when with body and soul; she longed to allow herself to be taken by the vortex. She wonders, too, what would have happened to her, if she had?

* * *

Ingrid did close her hand. She found the goatskin pouch in her pocket. She placed the stone in it. She returned it to her pocket. The red light was extinguished - totally. She was plunged into absolute darkness. It was the kind of utter blackness which made Ingrid wonder whether she had in fact gone blind. She could hear the urgent, quiet voices of her friends outside the room. In the terrifying dark she turned to face the point where she believed her escape route lay. By slow degrees, her eyes adjusted until she could dimly see red light from the gap at the top of the rock-pile.

At the same time she detected a sound from the other side of the table, behind her. It was the sound of scurrying, scuttling claws on stone; fast and purposeful. Thousands of claws. Stonestalkers! There was no doubt even in the darkness, that they were in pursuit of her, and they were coming, fast. Sheer fear gave her the strength and stamina to scale the twelve feet of rock faster than she would have believed possible. By the time she was half-way up, the largest stonestalkers were already attacking her boots with their scorpion-like tails. She had to kick them off repeatedly as she climbed. As she kept glancing back to see how close they were she was appalled by their size and number. The largest individuals were more than twice as big as the ones they had seen earlier. Continuing to kick out wildly as she climbed, she realised by the time she was near the top that they were poor climbers, and most were giving up the chase. As she reached the gap she could make out Ketu's anxious face at the other end of the narrow tunnel. The brave creature had managed to climb up the other side to watch out for her and was shining all three of their light pendants into the narrow tunnel to help her vision. He was calling out,

"Come on, Ingrid, come on! Quick, quick quick! Nearly there! Come on!"

He had to climb down to give Ingrid room to climb down herself, but he kept up a monologue of encouraging noises as she eased herself once again into the hideously small space, shuffling as fast as she could with all the strength left in her. She was hoping against hope that the stonestalkers could not make it that far. She was completely vulnerable in her crawling position, and these beasts looked big enough to kill. At last she was through. As she half fell, half scrambled back down, the two yeti grabbed her and as soon as she was low enough, Kol-pa took her in her arms and lay her gently onto the ground several yards from the rock-pile. She gave Ingrid another drink of water, and then, from a small vial which she had slung around her neck, a draught of something else, slightly sweet and wonderfully reviving.

"Oh, Ingrid, you did it! You're safe," exclaimed Kol-pa, "We didn't know about the stonestalkers – I'm so sorry, so sorry. And when you screamed, we didn't know if... You've had so much to bear, but you're safe and – you – you do still have it, don't you?"

Kol-pa had always seemed so calm and imperturbable. It was quite shocking to Ingrid to hear her sounding almost *human*. Without a word, Ingrid retrieved the pouch from her pocket and tried to give it to Kol-pa, but she shied away and would not touch it.

"No! I cannot take it – it's in the Prophecy! You must carry it all the way back, and *you* must give it to Mamo," said Kol-pa, holding up her palm gently to push the bag away.

"Alright, I didn't know," said Ingrid, feeling strangely pleased to keep it, "but perhaps now I've got it, you can tell me what on earth this Prophecy is. Well," she added, "once we're at a safe distance from the stonestalkers, that is."

"The stonestalkers are hopeless climbers, and besides, they are dim-witted. Once you have disappeared from sight, they forget about you. We have far greater dangers around us than stonestalkers. We dare not stop. We are not yet safe. Mamo will explain all to you when we return, I'm sure."

As they spoke, Ketu was holding both Ingrid's hands to pull her up to standing and she allowed herself to be pulled. Ingrid was secretly amazed at his strength. It was as though he was lifting up nothing more than a rag doll. He then continued to hold one of Ingrid's hands, standing to attention like an over-sized toddler on a nursery outing. When they stood together, he almost reached Ingrid's shoulder.

"Thank you, Ketu," she smiled before continuing to Kol-pa, "But, listen, do you think that Kra put the stonestalkers in there to kill me?"

"No, no," answered Kol-pa emphatically, "once you had taken the stone, it would be no use for him if you died in there. He has many ways to frighten you – as you have discovered – these are his attempts to win you over to his side through sheer terror. He needs you outside the sacred room with the Universe Stone. The true threat from Kra begins now. The fact that the stonestalkers were nesting in there was nothing to do with him, I'm certain of that. They probably found a crack to get in years ago, after the rock-fall made the walls unstable. Anyway, this is too much talk. We need to move!"

"Yes, but which way?"

"Ketu and I did explore a little way down one tunnel which would divert us from the Dragon Cave, but I just don't know if it will take us all the way out. I do not think we have many choices."

"Let's try it."

* * *

The new tunnel had a very gentle upward gradient, and was astonishingly straight and easy in comparison with their tortuous journey there. The yeti children were on edge, looking for any sight or sound of danger. Ingrid felt strangely unconcerned, as though this Kra character was just a silly myth. After all, she had done her job, hadn't she? She had confronted dragons, been exposed to mind-altering minerals, endured cuts, bruises, grazes, escaped venomous snakes and poisonous stonestalkers! Above all, she had the Universe Stone, and whatever that was, having it in her pocket made her feel invincible.

They passed through numerous caves, the walls of which were flecked with the gemstones they had already seen, but nothing to match the wonders of their outward journey. They were all quiet, which suited Ingrid. She wanted to think about the incredible experience of the vortex and keep it alive in her memory for as long as possible.

After a steeper ascent, they eventually came to a cave with about twelve or more tunnels running from it. The cave itself sloped upwards, and Kol-pa chose the tunnel at the highest point. It appeared to have more strata of blue and purple running through it, which Kol-pa saw as a positive sign.

As usual, Kol-pa went first. Just as Ingrid was about to enter, a vision shot into her mind. It was Mamo, as she had been in Ingrid's dream, standing to her full height, snarling and roaring in rage. Kol-pa was only just ahead. Ingrid grabbed her arm and whispered,

"Kol-pa, be careful!"

Kol-pa had obviously sensed something, too. She stopped and reached back to take Ingrid's hand. Ingrid reached back with her other hand to take Ketu's again. He was whimpering, also sensing that something was not as it should be. Kol-pa still had not moved. Clearly she was battling with an internal conflict: this way *smelled* of danger, yet it seemed to be the correct way out. If they tried a different route, they could be lost in a never-ending maze.

Finally, Kol-pa turned back to Ingrid and Ketu, mouthing the words,

"Keep close together and be quiet!"

They moved forward with extreme care. This tunnel was very short with an easy flat surface. It led after only about twenty yards into another cave. The entrance was wide and all three could walk in together, still holding hands. Ingrid, who had left her jacket and jumper way back in the tunnels, was now wearing only a thin cotton shirt on top. She was feeling unpleasantly shivery, but whether it was fear or cold, she could not tell. They were all wearing their light pendants, but they only illuminated a yard or so ahead. The cave was not supplied with much light from the weak threads of blue stone which ran across its walls.

Suddenly, from somewhere to their left, Ingrid was seized. It happened with such force and speed that the yeti children could not hold on to her. She screamed in shock and terror. Ketu shrieked in fear, clinging on to his sister. Ingrid could not see who held her, but she knew. The voice was Nepali but Ingrid still had the Speaking Stone in her pocket and could understand every vicious word.

"Hello, my friends. I see you are all wearing your Speaking Stones. It is important that we all understand each other. You have been very clever to come this far. What a shame it has all been for nothing. Your quest ends here. It's been such a tiring day. Just give me what I want and we can all go home to bed, can't we?"

Kra

Kra was holding Ingrid so tightly around the shoulders and chest she could barely breathe. She tried to twist her head to look at her captor, but he had such extraordinary strength that she was immobilised. Meanwhile, Kol-pa was gathering her wits, and her anger was rising. She seemed at that moment to grow in stature. She approached Kra, snarling.

"Oh no, I don't advise that, my dear mountain monkey," laughed Kra, "I can twist this little girl's scrawny neck as easily as a chicken's if you come any closer. I don't *want* to kill her, you understand – it might prove inconvenient – but if I have to, I will."

Kol-pa stopped moving, but continued to snarl. To any other human she would have looked very frightening indeed, but Kra was unmoved.

"Shall I tell you something, Ingrid?" he went on, squeezing her ribcage so hard she thought it would snap, "Your darling mother has had an accident. Oh, don't worry, she *probably* won't die. She had a fall, and her leg is badly cut. She and your father are resting in a tea-house nearby. She is being cared for there. Of course, it's a bad cut. Blood poisoning is always a possibility. All I have to do is go there tonight when they are all asleep. I can be very quiet, but you know that, don't you?" he laughed, "and I can be almost invisible. I can just sprinkle a tiny amount of powder on that cut, and a tragic death would follow. Sad, isn't it," he laughed again, coldly, and added with heavy sarcasm, "Such a lovely woman!"

As he spoke, Ingrid felt that her heart was being ripped from her chest, leaving a desolate and black hole of despair. She stopped struggling and became completely limp.

"I will do whatever you want me to, but *please* leave my mother," she pleaded.

"Just give me what I want."

Kra eased his grip sufficiently for Ingrid to reach her trouser pocket. She slowly took out the goatskin pouch as Kol-pa roared in frustration and anger,

"No!"

Kra snatched it and pushed Ingrid roughly aside, his eyes lighting up with greed. Ingrid fell to the ground landing painfully on her elbow and hip. The yeti did not move. Kra slowly opened the pouch. Ingrid hauled herself up, but then hardly dared breathe as she watched him.

As Kra allowed the stone to drop from the pouch into his left hand, the most appalling thing happened. As the stone dropped, it burned a hole straight through Kra's palm and fell to the ground. He stared in horror at the burning oval hole in his hand, his handsome face twisted in agony. He let out the most sickening and agonised scream Ingrid had ever heard in her life, falling to his knees, staring and staring in anguish. There was no blood coming from the wound: the searing heat from the stone had cauterised it. There remained just enough skin and bone for the fingers to hang on, but Ingrid was revolted by the sight. The smell of burning human flesh and bone was stomach-churning. Ingrid and the yeti were momentarily petrified with shock at what they were witnessing. Kra continued to howl, looking at his fingers hanging limply from what was left of his hand. Then they began to hear another sound: a deafening, thunderous rumbling. Kra's screams were causing a massive rock-fall somewhere in the caves, and the sound was drawing nearer. At the same time, the Universe Stone was beginning to pulsate. Despite what had just happened to Kra, Ingrid did an incredibly brave thing. She made a grab for the stone and threw it into the pouch. Kol-pa and Ketu also leapt forward, screaming at Ingrid,

"Come on!"

Ingrid, astonished that she was unharmed, shoved the pouch into her pocket, and with the yeti, she ran. As they were about to leave the cave, stones were already tumbling from the walls. Ingrid looked back at Kra. He was trying to get to his feet, but the cave floor was shaking and stones were falling around him. As he looked up at Ingrid in hatred and rage, his face still retained a classical beauty. His eyes reminded her of someone. If they were to leave him here, there was no doubt about his fate. She hesitated. Kol-pa was already running along her chosen tunnel as fast as her bulky form would allow. Ketu shoved Ingrid onwards, yelling,

"Run, or we die!"

Thinking again of her mother, she turned from Kra, and ran on, easily catching up with Kol-pa. She had no idea where they were going, or even if Kol-pa knew, but she followed in sheer blind terror, pursued by the booming sound of falling rocks, on and on, ever upward. She had no idea for how long they ran and stumbled through tunnel after tunnel, until finally Kol-pa shouted,

"I can see daylight!"

CHAPTER ELEVEN
The Fulfilment

Within twenty minutes they reached the surface. The way out was only just big enough for Kol-pa. Ketu and Ingrid had to muster all their remaining strength to push and pull her through. Now, at last, as the low sun streaked the sky with gorgeous swathes of orange and red, making the mountains glow, they could breathe in deep lungfuls of the sweet, breezy air. Now, all three of them lay still and silent, on soft dry grass in a small clearing surrounded by bare rock. Ketu and Ingrid lay near each other, flat on their backs in the sun; Kol-pa a little distance away, in some shade offered by the rise of a scrub-covered hill. The rumbling of the rocks below had ended. The only sound they could hear was that of the circling vultures in the foothills around them, calling to each other as though they suspected fresh meat was in the offing.

After a while, Ingrid began to hear another sound, much closer than the calling vultures. Somewhere between a purr and a growl; it was intermittent at about three or four second intervals. Ingrid's blood ran cold. Without a doubt it was the growl of a snow leopard.

She moved her head the smallest fraction and tried to turn her eyes to her left, near Ketu, from where the sound was coming. She could just make out Ketu's motionless shape, a yard or so away. He must be even closer to the cat than she was. The intermittent sound continued: grrrrrrrrrrrrrr – pause – grrrrrrrrrrrrr – pause – grrrrrrrrrrr. Despite her utter exhaustion and terror, she had to save Ketu. He would do the same for her. Perhaps if she could just throw some stones and yell at the top of her voice it would be enough to frighten it away. But snow leopards were fearless, ruthless killers. She imagined the leap…its hot jaws around her neck…the fatal incision…

However hopeless it was, she had to try to save Ketu. She leapt to her feet,

"Yaaaah! Get away! Get away!" she screamed, waving her arms frantically.

There was one more purring growl, then a snuffling grunt, as Ketu awoke in horror and also leapt to his feet, his enormous blue eyes like saucers.

"What? What?" he shouted, his brain still rising from a beautiful dream. He looked all around him, mystified. There was nothing there. Ingrid, too, scanned the horizon, then blushed deep red.

"Oh, sorry, I thought…"

"You thought Ketu's snoring was a snow leopard?" said Kol-pa, now sitting up and laughing, "You'll be seeing man-eating tigers and stampeding elephants next! There are no snow leopards in this area, and anyway, they'd never attack meh-teh! Come on, now, calm down and have a drink of water. Then you can hop on my back. We have a distance to go yet to return home. And no more scary snoring, Ketu!"

Ingrid felt a complete idiot as both yeti continued to laugh at her, so when Kol-pa passed her the water flask, she drank deeply to give her blush time to subside. She noticed that the two yeti children hardly drank at all. A bit like camels, she thought. When she had finished her drink she handed the flask back to Kol-pa, who slung it over her shoulder, then crouched down for Ingrid to hoist herself onto her back. They bounded away with Ketu close behind.

Dusk was transforming into night as they progressed fast over the sharp scree fields flanking the foothills to the left and right of them. Ingrid was feeling the cold, and grateful at least for the warmth of her friend's soft, furry back.

The gargantuan spikes of the Himalaya loomed before them, looking full of foreboding in the fading light. Ingrid's mind spun in a half-sleep over the extraordinary events of this single day in her life. An endless stream of doubts and "what ifs" cascaded through her exhausted brain. Above all, her fears were growing about her mother.

Kol-pa slowed a little and sighed,

"Ingrid, your mind is disturbed with worries about your mother. Slide off my back. That's it. Stand up. Take the little pieces of green stone from your pocket and hold them close to your heart for a moment. Listen, you must not worry. The villagers looking after your mother will tend the wound. It may not be serious and besides, Kra cannot get to her now."

"But what if he's not dead?" interrupted Ingrid, as she held the green stones tightly to her chest, still remembering Kra's terrible, anguished face..

"If he is not dead, then he has his own serious injuries to deal with. He will not be a threat to anyone for some time. Most importantly, the Universe Stone is out of his reach forever."

"But he could steal it from you, couldn't he?"

"After tomorrow, no, he could not. I know this does not make sense, but soon you will know all you need to know. We must get home – come on, up you get now."

Kol-pa could tell that Ingrid was far too tired for conversation, and she crouched down for her to climb back on, helped by Ketu, who was himself almost ready to drop. Ingrid did feel less anxious after holding the stones. She quickly returned them to her pocket, and gently patted the other pocket containing the Universe Stone as she resumed her place on the yeti girl's back. Kol-pa's words gave rise to even more questions in Ingrid's weary brain. Her mind formed the question, 'Why? What's happening tomorrow?', but she was asleep on the yeti's warm back before she could ask it.

The Fulfilment

When they arrived at the yeti cave, Ingrid was vaguely aware of Mamo and Nyima, waiting for them, but she could not help dozing off as soon as she was placed gently into Nyima's warm, motherly, sweet-smelling arms. In the back of her consciousness, she was aware of much whispering talk between the younger yeti and their mother and grandmother, but she was too befuddled with sleep to focus on their words. She was awoken by the blissful feeling of Nyima tending her many cuts, bruises and grazes, humming and singing as she did so. She was using some sharp-smelling oil which felt miraculously healing. Nyima had also placed the green and violet stones on Ingrid's solar plexus, just as Mamo had done the first time Ingrid entered the cave. Nyima gave her a plate of sweet bread and some tiny fruits like blueberries to eat, and placed several furry pillows under Ingrid's head to lift her to a half-sitting position so she could eat. She ate ravenously. Finally, Nyima helped her to wash her hands and face, and then said to her,

"It is time. You shall rest, but first you must take your part in the ceremony. Come with me."

She removed the stones from Ingrid's chest and held out her hand. Feeling shy and quiet, Ingrid rose and took the hand Nyima offered. As they walked along a well-lit corridor, Nyima told her to take the pouch out of her pocket. They entered a high-ceilinged room, at the far end of which sat Mamo, on a throne-like chair on a small raised platform. She wore around her neck a chain adorned with every colour of gemstone Ingrid had seen on her journey through the caves. At the centre of the chain was a red stone, far smaller than the Universe Stone, but obviously hewn from the same rock. Its light seemed to blaze like a fire against Mamo's heart.

Behind Mamo was a geometrical statue, about ten feet high, just like the one Ingrid had been climbing towards on the day she first met Kol-pa. The walls of the room were decorated with the same murals she had seen in the room that housed the Universe Stone.

The Stones and the Shaman

All around the room, some sitting on the floor, some raised up on cushions, were yeti of every size and age. There were several enormous scary-looking males, with strange cheek pouches and solemn expressions; there were about eight young adult females holding wide-eyed infants; there were Kol-pa and Ketu, who smiled when her eyes met theirs (Ketu gave a tiny wave); near them, another four or five children, perhaps siblings or cousins – a couple of whom were nudging each other naughtily. All eyes were watching Ingrid.

Although the yeti covered most of the floor space, a clear path had been left from the entrance across to Mamo's chair. Nyima nodded to Ingrid and let go of her hand. Ingrid knew what to do. It was as though she had dreamt this whole scene long ago. Slowly she walked up to Mamo and stepped up onto the platform. Mamo stood up. Ingrid opened the pouch and placed the Universe Stone in Mamo's waiting hand. Mamo held it to her heart so it touched its sister stone on her chain, then raised it up high above her head. Multi-coloured lights streamed from the Stone and filled the room as the yeti began to chant. The chant began softly and rose slowly in strength as the lights swirled and danced, until it seemed the whole earth must be full of light and song. The Stone was back where it belonged. Ingrid had fulfilled the Prophecy.

CHAPTER TWELVE
The Parting

Early the next morning, Ingrid was awoken from a fitful sleep of wild and troubling dreams by Ketu, bouncing up and down and jabbering excitedly. In a fog of sleepiness, she rolled across the bed and hauled herself up,

"OK, OK, I'm coming," she mumbled grumpily.

She had slept in her underwear and shirt, so she only had to grab her trousers from the floor and hoist them on. The aroma from her socks was not pleasant, but with no choice in the matter, she peeled them on. She then put her boots on with all speed to mask the smell. All the while Ketu stared, fascinated. He had never seen the process of dressing before.

He grabbed her hand and took her outside to the latrine she had visited the night before; extraordinarily clean and well hidden from view. He left her there for an appropriate time, then brought her a small quantity of mercifully warm water in an ivy wood bowl, for washing. To Ingrid's surprise, he also gave her a large bar of soap. It was greenish-cream in colour and roughly oblong. 'Yeti use *soap?*' she thought, smiling to herself. She put it to her nose. It smelled of sweet herbs and something else, like olive oil. He also provided a much-needed comb. Made of bone or horn, it was really too wide-toothed for Ingrid's fine, silky hair, but it was better than nothing, she thought.

Her wash in the cool, fresh mountain air, surrounded by birdsong was delightful. After washing, she realised that in fact, all her clothes were definitely smelly. In the bright sun, she could now see that they were also ripped and filthy. Even worse, back in the deep tunnels, she had lost her jumper (which had been knitted lovingly by her grandmother) and her jacket (which had been bought specially for this trip). Her parents would be furious. Her parents! Her thoughts flew back to her mother and all those dark worries about her injury. As if that were not bad enough, they would be frantic with worry about her. They would probably be making attempts to contact the British Consulate to declare her missing. She dreaded the horrendous row that would ensue on her return. She realised she needed to invent a superbly convincing story to explain her absence. As she racked her brain, Ketu returned with Nyima and Kol-pa, who was carrying Ingrid's rucksack (still, she thought ruefully, containing her *un-used* drawing materials).

"We have come to say thank you and good-by, Ingrid," began Nyima, placing a small blanket around Ingrid's shoulders, like a shawl. She was grateful for it. The weather was on the change and the cold breeze seemed to eat into her bones. Ingrid then took her rucksack and managed with some awkwardness to manoeuvre the straps over the shawl. Nyima continued,

"We know you are anxious about your mother and wish to return now as soon as possible. You will find food in your rucksack to eat on the way. Now, I have to tell you, we cannot reward you for your bravery, but you may find that your journey in the caves has changed you in ways that may help you – and others – in the future. We hope your memories of us will stay with you, and one day, you will tell all your people about us, and about how you saved us."

"I wasn't always very brave, actually," said Ingrid, feeling her cheeks turn red.

"You were! You were!" shouted Ketu, grabbing her round the waist for a hefty squeeze.

Ingrid laughed as she was almost knocked over by Ketu's enthusiasm, and said,

"Thank you, Ketu, and so were you! But, Nyima, there's still so much I don't know…what *was* the Prophecy?"

"Oh," said Nyima, "I suppose you deserve to know that. Be patient and I will tell you."

"The first of the Wise Ones, Yangchen, had the gift of clairvoyance long before we discovered the Stones of Power in these mountains. She foresaw that humans would multiply way beyond their ability to care for themselves or for the planet. She foresaw that as they multiplied, they would grow in belligerence and greed. She foresaw that they would destroy many species of animal, bird, fish and plant. She foresaw the possibility that they would destroy the planet and themselves along with it."

Ingrid began to interrupt, her face now red with anger.

"No, Ingrid, you wanted to hear this. Allow me to finish. I am telling you as briefly as I can. Many of the details of Yangchen's Prophecy have already occurred in exactly the way she predicted. If I began to list the creatures already extinct due to the thoughtless and selfish activity of humans, you would be listening to me for a very long time."

"Yangchen also told us that we would discover and guard planet Earth's greatest secret: the Stones. They have helped us to live a peaceful, happy and harmless life here for many years, but Yangchen knew that one day a man would discover our secret and try to steal it. If he were to succeed, this would mean the destruction of humankind, of the meh-teh and of the Earth itself. The Stones are too powerful to be used in ignorance."

"The rock-fall that occurred in the caves many years ago has kept the Universe Stone safe, but it also meant that we ourselves could not use it to escape from this planet. It was impossible for us to move the rubble from the rock-fall without the risk of the collapse of the whole chamber. It was too unstable. And even the smallest of the meh-teh would have been too big to crawl through into the sacred room."

"Yangchen knew that *you* would help us. She said that a green-eyed girl from the West would arrive at the auspicious time for us to leave – the time when the stones were in most danger. She said *the girl would be related to the very one who would try to steal the Universe Stone from us.*"

"What!" gasped Ingrid in horror and disbelief, "How could I possibly be related to Kra? That's utterly ridiculous! It's nonsense!"

Ingrid tried to laugh, but her laughter sounded dry and hollow. The yeti children were looking on, impassively, giving the impression that they were already well aware of this. Nyima smiled,

"Perhaps you should ask your mother about her grandparents some time."

Ingrid was speechless with confusion. Related to that monster? How could she, a girl from Cornwall, be related to a shaman from Nepal? It was ludicrous, and yet everything else Yangchen had said…

She turned her back on the others for a moment, her arms folded, staring across at Everest. It was rapidly becoming covered in cloud. To Ingrid now, it looked a fearful place. She wanted to go. She turned back again to Nyima, who continued gently,

"Now, my dear, dear girl, you must go. Because of your mother's accident, your parents have not yet returned to camp and do not know you have been away, but your porters are terrified that they will be in serious trouble when they find out. For their sakes, you must hurry back."

"Listen. There is a plateau which you can see from your camp when you look to the West. Do you know it?"

"Yes. It's beautiful."

"Tonight, when the sun sets, look to the plateau," said Nyima.

The Parting

All of a sudden, Ingrid felt so tired, confused and sad, that she was close to tears. She just managed to choke out the words,

"Of course, I will."

Kol-pa, who had remained quiet while Nyima had been speaking, now placed her long arms around Ingrid,

"Thank you, friend of the meh-teh, and friend to me, always. Don't forget to make some drawings of us! Good-bye, Ingrid."

They hugged each other so breath-stoppingly tight that Ingrid did momentarily wonder if the food in her rucksack would be horribly squashed. Then Ketu joined in the hugs,

"Good-bye, Ingrid. Remember, snow leopards don't snore!"

Nyima spoke again, "You have to make your own way back, now, Ingrid, but first you must give me all the stones in your pocket."

Unquestioningly, and with a sense of relief, Ingrid did so. After more cuddles from the younger yeti, Nyima, too, hugged Ingrid briefly then released her to go on her journey.

She began to march. After two or three minutes, she turned to wave to her friends. They were still there, grouped like a Victorian family photograph. They waved back. The next time she looked, they were gone.

Ingrid's march soon became an amble. She felt massively let down, dejected, disappointed. Had she gone through all that just to wander back to the camp as though nothing had happened? She had been a heroine, hadn't she? Now she just faced a huge row with Tshering while she placated him with a lie she hadn't even invented yet. And far, far worse, her mother was sick and injured. The more she thought about it, the more a black hole of despair grew in her heart. She kicked stones viciously as she trudged along.

Her stomach emitted a loud complaint. She remembered the packed breakfast in her rucksack. She found a suitable rock and sat down, hugely cheered by the thought of food. The meal was carefully packed in thin material similar to muslin, and placed considerately in a separate compartment from her sketchpad. Nyima had given her some savoury rolls, the outer casings of which were made of a scrumptious cross between bread and pastry. The inner parts of the rolls were filled with a spicy mixture of delicious vegetables. She ate gratefully, allowing her mind to rest from all its unpleasant thoughts while she concentrated on the food and studied the view. As soon as she had finished she hoisted on her rucksack once more, and marched on.

She eventually reached the spot where she had first met Kolpa. As she rounded the bend to begin the steep descent, she saw a figure sitting on the same rock she had been seated on. The figure turned. It was Sonam!

CHAPTER THIRTEEN
Friend and Relations

He began speaking at once in his educated English,

"Ingrid, you must come back to the camp as quickly as you can. I have made up a story about you, that you lost your way and I have told Tshering that I found you and you have stayed the night with my family. I know everything that has happened."

"How on earth do you know?"

"I saw you for a moment when your mind's eye was beginning to open up down in the tunnels. I knew you were in very great danger – I tried to warn you. I had to leave Ketsun to go for the yaks – he will return with them tomorrow with another boy. I came back here to help you."

"But how could you see me? How did you know I was in danger? How do you know about Kra?"

Sonam sighed. "Let us walk as we talk."

As they began the descent, he continued,

"Kra is – perhaps I should say, was (we do not know, do we?) – my uncle, my mother's half-brother. I am ashamed to tell you that he was a member of my family. We are all ashamed. My maternal grandmother was the daughter of a shaman. She married a shaman herself and Kra was their son. After Kra's father died, my grandmother married again, this time to a Sherpa. My mother and all of her sisters and brothers are the children of that second marriage."

Ingrid felt her head was ready to explode. She pushed her hair away from her face,

"Sonam – I've just been told that *I* am in some way related to Kra! This is all too much for me to take in! Are *we* related, too? I feel as though I'm going completely mad!"

As she looked at Sonam, she then blurted out,

"You look like Kra! I should have realised!"

Sonam looked embarrassed.

"Actually, we both, Kra and I, resemble my great-grandfather, Kra's grandfather. To be like Kra is nothing to be proud of. I am like him in another way. I have the shamanic powers, and that is how I knew of your danger. I knew the first time I saw you, exactly who you were."

"So how do I fit in to all this?"

"It is not as extraordinary as it sounds. I will tell you as simply as I can. We share the same great-grandfather."

"What!" said Ingrid, stopping in her tracks for a moment to stare at Sonam, "But you said your great-grandfather was a shaman!"

Sonam stopped with her and stared back.

"Ingrid, please *listen*! Our great-grandfather was *British.* He was an explorer, and what you would call an eccentric. Did I say that word correctly?"

Ingrid nodded. They resumed their walk.

"Well, he believed – rightly as it seems now – that he had special powers, and he believed that by travelling to the East, he could find out more about them. He read all he could on the subject of…"

Ingrid helped him out as he struggled for the word, "Telepathy? Clairvoyance?"

"Yes, thank you, clairvoyance. Anyway, he decided on Nepal as the best place to learn more about the way in which he was different. He loved Nepal and quickly decided to settle here. He married a local girl, and their first child, a daughter, was the woman who became your grandmother."

"Grandmother! I can't believe it! I'd never have guessed! But how…"

"Wait, I haven't finished! Her father (our great-grandfather, remember!) felt his daughter should be brought up in Britain. So he returned her to England, to be raised by his own parents. That is all I know of her. I am told that our great-grandfather regretted losing his first-born daughter for the rest of his life. That is why all the later children (including *my* grandmother) were brought up in Nepal. So, you see, I am a little bit British, and you are a little bit Nepalese!"

"My head's spinning with all this! Our grandmothers were actually sisters, right? I'll need to think about how I am related to Kra – not that I want to think about it, and besides…"

"I know. You did the right thing back in the caves. Believe me; he would have killed to have that Stone. He must have known exactly who you were, but - have no doubt about it - he would not have hesitated to kill you. It sickened him to think that he had British blood and yet he did not have the riches that he believed all British people have."

"He said he would kill my mother," said Ingrid staring at the ground.

"He would have done anything to possess the Universe Stone. But in the end it could not fall into the wrong hands because this is not the way of the Universe: it seeks always to create and re-create, not destroy. The meh-teh say the Universe Stone is the heart of our planet," he turned to Ingrid and smiled, "I wonder what will become of us all without a heart?"

They were now within a hundred yards of the camp. Tshering and Pasang were chatting quietly over the fire. As usual, a large pan of tea was boiling steadily over it. Before Ingrid could ask what he meant by his last comment, Sonam said in a hushed voice,

"Remember not to talk to me! Oh, and good luck!"

"Thank you – *cousin!"* replied Ingrid. The word sent a surge of happiness through her and she grinned broadly. Then, as she approached the waiting Sherpas, she prepared herself for a major row.

CHAPTER FOURTEEN
The Plateau

There was no row. Tshering and Pasang had evidently been extremely anxious, both about Ingrid and her mother. When she arrived at the camp with Sonam, the two Sherpas' faces were full of joy, relief and welcome. She thought Pasang was going to cry,

"Miss Ingrid, Miss Ingrid, we are so happy to see you! You must never disappear from us again! You are very, very lucky that Sonam found you. You stay with your Sherpas now – oh yes! - and no more running away!"

She felt remorse and guilt for having been the cause of so much worry. She even suspected that Pasang's hair had turned whiter in her twenty-four hours' absence. While Sonam immediately busied himself, Ingrid was presented with food and drink as though she were a visiting princess. Tshering did look disapprovingly at Ingrid's bedraggled appearance and eyed her yeti shawl with suspicion, but he made no comment. She asked Pasang about her mother's injury.

"There are no bones broken, but it is a bad wound – *here*," he pointed to his left calf muscle, "and it is deep. The people in the nearest tea-house to where she fell are caring for her until she is well enough to travel. It is more than two hours' walk from here. Your father is still searching and collecting, but it is slow and hard for him with only Pemba to help him." He paused, "Miss Ingrid, we did not tell them about you being lost. We did not want to worry them."

Ingrid felt immediate annoyance with her father for carrying on working despite her mother being seriously injured. So typical! Then a kinder part of her mind came up with the notion that maybe it was what her mother wanted. Also, if they didn't go home with enough rare and exotic new species, they wouldn't receive the money they so badly needed.

"Look, Pasang, I am really, really sorry. I won't cause you any more trouble, I promise," she looked pleadingly into Pasang's dark brown eyes set in their landscape of innumerable folds and wrinkles, "I wonder, would you mind *please* taking me to my mother now?"

Sonam had been very quiet all this time, but now he came over and joined in, speaking to Pasang and Tshering in Sherpa. As Tshering replied crossly, Ingrid found to her heart-stopping amazement that she *knew* what had been said – *without the Speaking Stone!* Sonam had said he would take her there himself this afternoon, if they liked. Tshering replied - roughly translated – that he most certainly would not; he (Sonam) had work to do and besides, he (Tshering) did not want Sonam becoming too familiar with Western girls, especially not such an unruly, uncivilised one as this.

As Ingrid's head reeled from the shock, Pasang chuckled at the exchange between Sonam and Tshering and then spoke to Ingrid in English,

"Miss Ingrid, you cannot go back there today. It is past noon. You could not go there and back before dark, and the villagers in the tea-house do not have room for you to stay. They are poor people and it is hard for them to have your parents there, although they will be well paid for this. I will take you there tomorrow. By then your mother may be a little better. Today, you must stay here and rest. Tomorrow, we set out early for the tea-house and," he added in a kind tone, "Please do not worry yourself about your mother."

As Pasang spoke the words 'there and back before dark', Ingrid remembered that of course she could not leave the camp before dark. She had to '*look to the plateau at sunset.* She had made a promise to Nyima and she hoped that if she kept that promise it would reveal to her the true purpose of her quest to retrieve the Stone. She desperately missed her mother and had a dark ache of anxiety whenever she thought of her, but whatever her feelings, she knew her mother would want her to keep a promise.

"OK," she replied, "I *am* tired. I have some drawings I need to do, so I'll go and rest in my tent for a while and sort out my sketch book."

Although this had just been something to say, she realised as she said it, that she must indeed start to draw. She had to record in her sketchbook everything she had seen over the last two days. She needed to get the images down as soon as possible before her memories began to fade. If only she'd taken the camera! How could she have been so unforgivably, idiotically stupid?

At once, she returned to her tent. She found a comfortable way to sit at the entrance with the flaps open, so that the angle of the midday light was perfect. With rapt concentration she worked. Before long she had produced accurate representations of Kol-pa, Ketu, Mamo, Nyima, the yeti cave, the tunnels. But there were other images that needed to be recorded. She recalled the terrifying faces of the dragons, the horrible semi-transparent stonestalkers, the hideous snakes, the nightmare faces of the demons and – Kra. Her relative, Kra. She recalled the horror on his face as the Universe Stone dropped straight through his hand like a hot knife through butter. She recalled his agonised look at her as she left the cave. Could she draw those terrible images? Suddenly, she felt utterly drained. She needed to think about those things some other time. She closed the book, entered the tent, removed her boots, lay on her sleeping bag, and instantly, slept.

A polite voice was calling.

"Miss Ingrid, supper will be ready in half an hour, please."

Ingrid awoke with an unpleasant jolt, emerging from the deepest, dreamless sleep.

"OK, Tshering, thank you," she managed to call, before her consciousness drifted down to somewhere close to sleep again. As random thoughts wafted lazily through her head, the smells of Tshering's mouth-watering food caught her nose and she leapt up,

"Oh no! Supper! It must be sunset!"

Frantically, she heaved on her heavy boots and rushed off to find Sonam. He simply had to be there with her. She needed to share this with him. Luckily, he was some distance from Tshering and Pasang at the other side of the camp, feeding the yaks. The sun was sinking rapidly; huge paint-strokes of orange and pink were splashed wildly across the sky. The plateau could be seen from a vantage point only two hundred yards away.

"Sonam! There's no time to explain! We have to go to where we can see the plateau! Something is going to happen. Please come right now!"

Ingrid tugged his arm.

"I know. I was waiting for you," he smiled, "let's go."

He took her hand to help her across the rocks in the fading light. As they reached the viewpoint, they could see all the yeti already gathered on the high lonely place. From where Ingrid and Sonam stood, even the enormous males were no bigger than Ingrid's hand. Mamo was at the centre of the group. Ingrid could just see sparkling around her neck the same chain she had worn the night before, at the ceremony.

The sun was about to disappear behind the mountains when the red of the sky paled against the red light now surging from Mamo's right hand as she held the Universe Stone aloft. The humming Ingrid had heard at the stone altar had returned. The light was turning into a vortex, growing larger and larger until it embraced the whole group. It was dizzying to watch. Ingrid tried to make out the figures of the yeti within the swirling light. She thought she saw Ketu. She thought she saw him wave. As the sun disappeared, there was a blinding flash from which Ingrid had to shield her eyes. When she opened them again, the yeti were gone.

They had been her special friends. They had been through nightmares together; saved each others' lives. Now they were gone from her forever. How could they leave her?, she thought angrily. There was no-one now to share her memories of those events. Would there come a time when she herself would doubt that they had ever happened? Why did they have to go? Surely the world wasn't that bad a place?

Ingrid and Sonam continued to stand for some time looking towards the empty plateau. Ingrid became aware that she was still holding Sonam's hand. She didn't let go.

Ingrid was crying silently. Sonam turned to her,

"You don't *know* that it's forever."

"Do you think they will come back one day?" she asked, hastily wiping her eyes with her sleeve.

"I like to think so. Let's believe they will."

"Sonam, where do you think they've gone?"

"Who knows? The Universe must have many planets not so different from our own."

"Are they really the last yeti?"

"Yes. They had no choice. If they had remained here they would have died out, just like so many other creatures in the history of the Earth. It is up to you now to keep their memory; however you can, although who can tell whether anyone will believe you? Anyway, come on, we must go! We don't want you getting into any more trouble."

"No, nor you!" she smiled, "You shouldn't be mixing with an uncivilised Western girl like me!"

The first stars were appearing as they turned to go back.

"We'd better go back separately," said Sonam, letting go of Ingrid's hand, "or I *will* be in trouble. Go! I'll join you in a few minutes."

* * *

Supper was uneventful. Pasang chatted away, partly in his strongly accented English, partly in Sherpa. At one point Tshering commented on how lucky Miss Ingrid had been to see such a very beautiful Himalayan sunset this evening. 'Yes, very lucky indeed!' thought Ingrid smiling to herself and not daring to catch Sonam's eye. Ingrid continued to be amazed that she could understand Tshering and Pasang in both languages.

Her experience with the strata of Speaking Stone appeared to have caused some miraculous shift in her brain. But it was the miracle of the vortex which carried away the yeti that dominated her thoughts. Her new-found linguistic skill seemed no more to her than a magician's trick. It would not be until later in her life that she would come to value that particular gift. She remained quiet, staring into the flames of the camp fire, as a flickering, shadowy reminder of the blinding red light.

CHAPTER FIFTEEN
Miracle

The next morning, Tshering called her early for a hasty breakfast so they could depart on time to visit her parents. Tshering had changed his mind about Sonam. He would now come with them because they needed to take a yak with them, laden with supplies for the family who were caring for Mrs. Wildsmith, and as her means of transport to return to camp. Sonam was to lead the yak. It was windy and cool. Ingrid was grateful for the change in temperature. She was too exhausted to walk in the heat. However, the wind depressing, and she kept thinking of her yeti friends, gone forever.

They set out, trudging generally downward, through landscapes purple with what Ingrid thought were rhododendrons. Ingrid's knees ached from the constant downhill movement. The yak was in a bad mood and needed much encouragement. Tshering, despite his age, kept bounding on ahead to check the route. This gave Ingrid occasional moments to question Sonam,

"Sonam, I still don't really know – what is a shaman?

Sonam turned to Ingrid whilst keeping tight control of the unwilling yak,

"I'll try to explain, but even though I have the powers, I do not always understand them! Shamans are a little like your priests or – you have some other word…"

"We have a vicar in our village – is that what you mean?"

"Maybe. I don't know much about your priests or vicars! Anyway, a shaman can actually be a man or a woman. We have the power to speak to deities, to heal some illnesses, to change the weather, and of course, some clairvoyance," he paused to persuade the yak down a steep incline, "Come on, you can do it! That's it!"

he turned again to Ingrid, "People ask their shaman about auspicious dates for weddings or naming ceremonies. Also, one very important job is to help people when they die to make the…what word?...I don't know!...when they move on to their next life. A shaman can tell the relatives when it is the right time for the cremation of the dead person."

"And what do you think turned Kra to evil?"

"My family believe he was possessed by a demon. So we could say that he could not help becoming evil. The faces you saw in your dreams and in the rocks were not just images in your mind. They were wrathful deities called up by Kra. They could not possess you because you did not believe in them."

"But what if…"

"Sshh, here comes Tshering."

Ingrid hastily moved away from Sonam to look as though she was walking by herself. There was one more brief moment to speak before they arrived at the tea-house.

"How is it that you speak such good English? At first I didn't think you could speak it at all," said Ingrid, shyly.

"My – *our*- great-grandfather made sure that all his children spoke perfect English. Even though he loved Nepal, and the Nepalese and Sherpa people, he was sensible enough to realise that it would help his children to know English. He lived to be a very old man, and he taught most of his grandchildren English, including my mother, who taught me."

"What was his name?"

"His English name was William Douglas. As he was born on a Tuesday, he adopted the Sherpa name, Mingma."

"William Douglas," Ingrid said the name over to herself quietly, then studying the ground before her, she asked, "Can you," she hesitated, feeling herself blush, "I don't mean to be rude, but can you *write* English?"

"It is not a rude question!" laughed Sonam, "Yes, I can write. Although of course, we do not always have very much paper at home, nor many pens or pencils."

"It's just that we'll be leaving here soon, and I know you're not coming with us to Kanchenjunga. Well, we are related and everything and I really need somebody to talk to about all that's happened. You seem to know so much about the yeti and the Stones. There's still so much I'd like to know about my family, too, so I just wondered if we could…maybe write to each other," she blurted, now a deep ruby red.

"Oh yes," grinned Sonam, "I think we could do that."

Ingrid grinned broadly back at him as Tshering returned again to take the yak from Sonam as they reached the tea-house. Tshering eyed them suspiciously.

* * *

As they arrived at the tea-house, Mr. Wildsmith, looking worn and tired, rushed up to greet his daughter. He actually hugged her. Already filled with the warm glow of her new-found friendship with Sonam, it was easy for her to return her father's hug.

"Ingrid! At last!"

"Hello, Dad, I…"

"Thank goodness you're here. It will mean so much to your mother to see you now…Ingrid," he gently pushed her away from him to look her in the eye, "she really is quite unwell. Go straight in."

Ingrid went inside, alone. The house had one large room roughly divided by a curtain into kitchen space and sleeping space. Her mother was on a low wooden bed topped with a very old, lumpy looking mattress. She had a sheet and blankets over her, but her injured left leg was uncovered. It was badly swollen, heavily bandaged and elevated by a pillow. Ingrid was shocked by her frail appearance. She looked exhausted and could not hide from Ingrid that she was in pain. Ingrid steeled herself against her feelings as she approached the bed, thrusting her hands deep into her trouser pockets. She felt something sharp right in the bottom of one of them. She picked it up between her fingers and briefly examined it: a shard of dark green stone. She should have given all the stones back to Nyima…

She bent down to hug her mother. Ingrid was panicked to feel how hot she was on this cool day. Her mind flew back to Kra's words, *'blood poisoning is always a possibility'*. There was clearly a serious infection.

"Mummy, I've missed you so much," she said gulping back her emotions, "How are you feeling now?"

"Hello, darling. Well, it is still painful, but I think it's slowly getting better. It's so lovely to see you again."

With the little strength she could muster, she hugged her daughter back. As she lay back on the bed again and momentarily closed her eyes, Ingrid quickly took the shard of stone and, hardly daring to breathe, placed it lightly on the bandaged leg. She then gently eased a corner of the sheet over the stone to hold it in place. Her mother's eyes remained closed. She gave a short outward breath, and suddenly took on a more peaceful look. She was utterly motionless. For a few heart-wrenching seconds, Ingrid thought – no – her eyes slowly opened again.

"Do you know, Ingrid, I feel so much better just seeing you here. I think I'll have a little sleep now."

As her mother closed her eyes once more, Ingrid quietly left the room.

The couple, Yeshe and Lhamu, who lived in the tea-house, provided a lunch of the usual staple: rice, dhal and the most mouth-watering spicy pickles for Ingrid, her father and the Sherpas. They ate enjoyably with their fingers, scooping up the dhal with the sticky rice. The meal was followed by endless cups of Nepali tea. Sonam and Ingrid tactfully avoided looking at each other and stayed quiet. The adults spoke in hushed tones of the likely prognosis for Mrs. Wildsmith, all doing their best to sound optimistic and hopeful.

The tiny woman of the house, Lhamu, went in to see if Mrs. Wildsmith wanted a drink. Two minutes later she came rushing out, speaking very loudly and very fast in Nepali, and gesturing Mr. Wildsmith and Ingrid to come in. Ingrid's father's face turned ashen with dread. Ingrid, who had understood what had been said, raced in first to remove the stone from her mother's leg before it was discovered.

Her mother was sitting up, looking cheerful and alert. Her hazel eyes were clear and youthful again. Ingrid managed to remove the green stone by pretending to straighten her mother's sheets. She sneaked it carefully back into her pocket. Lhamu brought Mrs. Wildsmith a cup of tea and a small plate of rice and dhal.

"Thank you Ingrid, dear, that's much better," said her mother, happily, "And thank you so much, Lhamu, I am absolutely *ravenous.*"

Ingrid's father looked completely flabbergasted by his wife's miraculous recovery. She applied herself to the urgent task of eating, then said between mouthfuls,

"David, do you know, I started feeling better the moment Ingrid arrived! I think I will be well enough to go back to the camp tomorrow."

Mr. Wildsmith gently felt his wife's forehead.

"Do you know," he said, smiling at Ingrid, "I think you may be right."

THE END

Printed in the United Kingdom by
Lightning Source UK Ltd., Milton Keynes
136599UK00001B/438/P

9 781849 231312